LOST PERFECT KISS

A Crown Creek Novel

THERESA LEIGH

❀ Created with Vellum

To Anna.
Internet BFFs are the best BFFs. You really saved my butt on this one, which is a problem because now I'm COMPLETELY dependent on you. Sorry, that's just the way it is.
#NanaVivi4Lyfe

And I'm damned if I do and I'm damned if I don't

So here's to drinks in the dark at the end of my road

And I'm ready to suffer and I'm ready to hope

It's a shot in the dark and right at my throat

- Florence and the Machine - 'Shake It Off'

Chapter One

GABE

I was addicted to watching myself die.

My heart raced loud enough to drown out the sound of my breath coming faster. It felt like a hit of the purest dope I'd ever tried.

I was an addict now.

"I'm Gabriel King!" I shouted into the camera. "And I'm the King of Pain!"

A hot rush of adrenaline spiked in my veins just hearing the words. I could still feel it. The day was burned into my skin like some kind of fucked-up brand mark.

"Let's do this!" my image shouted at me.

I hovered my finger over the pause button. This was where I should stop. Right here. It wasn't healthy to keep watching. I knew this, which was why I kept my obsession secret. It was an addiction and I'd already been through that hell and come out the other side.

But the four walls of the room did their pulsing thing again, like they wanted to close in on me. A crawling sensation twisted under my skin, the one that always made me want to leap from my bed. The only thing that worked when this happened was finding a distraction.

One more time. I needed to watch just one more time.

There I was at the Perrine Bridge in Twin Falls Idaho—fifteen hundred feet above the Snake River twisting like a blue ribbon below us—hooked up to all my wires and mics. The day before, we'd rehearsed the jump and it had been the most wild rush I'd felt. Soaring like a fucking bird.

I remembered how I'd felt right then, in that moment before the jump. Impatient. All the delays and safety checks were just killjoys trying to piss all over my fun. I just wanted to *do* it, while my blood was still hot and thumping in my veins. I wanted to feel that same rush again, and was pissed at my safety guy for wanting to do another check. Again. Like, what the fuck? I knew what to do. We knew what to do, so let's fucking do it.

You could see it all over my face. Feeling fucking invincible, I'd grinned at the camera and given a stupid thumbs up. "Woo!" I shouted on the screen.

I glanced up, checking to see that I was alone in the house, and turned down the volume.

Then I hit pause.

Was it crazy to want to re-live the moment? Was I insane for wanting to see it all go wrong, over and over again? What the hell kind of rush could I possibly get from watching my own body slamming into the rocks? What sick pleasure did I get from watching myself go stiff, then limp, before gently floating down as lifeless as a puppet dangling from the strings of my parachute?

If I sat down with a shrink, they'd probably be able to come up with some deep-seated, deep-rooted reason for why I kept watching the video. But I was done with the psychoanalysis. I'd done more than a life's share of it in rehab, dragging through the pain and pulling it back up to feel it again.

That's what this was. Rehab. My own little personal, fucked-up form of rehab, the way only Gabe King could do it. It wasn't addiction at all.

Definitely not.

I half-believed my own lie as I propped the tablet up on my stomach. Then I took a deep breath—as deep as I could until the sharp pain in my ribs stopped me—and pressed play.

"Let's fucking do it!" the little me shouted from the tablet.

Here in the bed, my stomach dropped. Because now that I'd watched it at least a hundred times, I could see it in an instant. I'd fucking hurried my safety guy along, and there it was on screen. The evidence. He'd only glanced at how my chute was packed, without folding and refolding it one last time.

"Ready!" the camera guy shouted. The little me grinned. My heart raced in anticipation of the hit.

On the bed, my body twitched.

Onscreen, I jumped.

As I fell, the wind was so loud in my ears, I couldn't hear anything. But I could feel. All the protective gear I was wearing felt like cheating. I was flying and I wanted to be naked. I wished I could feel that wind on my skin, let the rush of it scour away the topmost layer until I was raw and red as a newborn baby.

I'd pulled my chute at the right moment. Here in the room, I closed my eyes as I remembered what happened next. Felt it. The horrible drag to the side as the wind caught me. My chute was rotated ninety degrees, sending me perpendicular to the canyon instead of parallel. The vortex of updrafts that close to the wall caught me almost instantly, like the hand of a giant bully dragging me off into an alley to beat the shit out of me.

It looked like it, too, there on the screen. I whipped around like an invisible giant had gotten ahold of me, spinning me around and dashing me against the canyon wall.

That was my old self. The me I used to be died right there. That first body-breaking slam into the rocks was the end of my old life. Thanks to the pause button, I could pinpoint the time of death down to the second.

Onscreen, stuff was still happening. "Oh, shit!" The cameraman said and everything went shaky.

Whatever Internet ghoul got ahold of this footage then did some fancy editing, splicing in the feed from my helmet cam. This allowed me to see what I couldn't remember, because that first collision with the canyon wall had knocked me out cold. But thanks to the video, I now knew that I was fucking lucky my chute didn't get tangled, because then I would have dropped like a stone. It remained caught in the updraft, the harness like a pendulum sending me slamming into the wall again and again, but not down. No. The swinging momentum of my broken body finally allowed it to escape the updraft and the feed leveled out as I floated out gently into the middle of the canyon again.

Everything was eerily silent on the video now. I couldn't even hear my own breathing. My head had fallen so the helmet tracked the canyon floor, the river flowing below me completely undisturbed. For a moment, everything seemed almost peaceful. Like I really had died and was now floating like a ghost.

Then from off camera came the sounds of the Jeep speeding to my rescue, a crew member calling my name. The last bits of video were just a shot of the sky and then it was over. Gabe King was dead and this new thing, this strange, broken person was born in his place.

I hurried to tuck the tablet away when I heard my mother's voice. She stormed into the sunroom where my hospital bed was set up, her cellphone shoved up against her ear, and she caught me as I slid the tablet under the sheets. Her mouth twisted. "Not again," she mouthed at me, but then her attention was caught by something the person on the other end said. "He still needs help doing everything," she hissed, and if there's a more emasculating thing in the world than lying in a hospital bed while your mother argues with someone about how you can't piss by yourself, I shudder to even imagine it. "The nurse needs to stay on another week at least. Until he gets onto crutches and even after that."

My older brother Jonah appeared, here for his daily visit. He'd moved into his fiancée's house while I was in the hospital, but came over every day to help me get into my chair. I shushed him with a look and he immediately started eavesdropping on Mom as well.

"Private nursing is covered under our plan, I know it is." She paused and listened. "Right but full recovery hasn't happened yet. He slammed into the side of a mountain!"

"Canyon," I corrected under my breath. My mom glared at me. Then her eyes widened at whatever they said and she abruptly stabbed the button to hang up. "Why do we even have health insurance?" she asked the air.

"So Ana's done?" I asked. "Can't say I'm too broken up about that."

"I know she wasn't the friendliest nurse in the world, but she was a big help around here." I hated how frazzled my mom looked. I also hated that it was because of me. It was enough to make a guy want to start drinking again.

No. I took a deep breath and tried to smile. "Mom, it's fine. I can get around great in the wheelchair now."

"No." She shook her head. "You still need help, Gabe." She huffed a sigh and then her mind went to work, the same organizational skills she put into place running a household with five kids. "I guess that's what I'm here for, though, right?"

Oh shit. "Mom. No."

Her glare was withering. "I'm your mother, Gabriel."

"I know." I tried to sit up straighter, hard to do in this fucking bed. "Which is why I'm not letting you give me a fucking sponge bath. Those days are over."

"Gabriel, I used to diaper your little weewee..."

Jonah snorted as I cried out in horror. "Jesus Christ, Mom!" I tried clap my hands over my ears and inadvertently grunted at the pain in my still-healing ribs.

Her face softened. "Gabe, you need help."

I looked from her to my brother and shook my head. "You guys have done enough. It's not your job to take care of me."

"But we can make it someone's job," Jonah piped up.

He looked at my mom and then at me and I could tell he was asking permission to go on. I had to give the guy credit, he was really working on not just steamrollering over everyone with his ideas. I credited his fiancée Ruby for that change.

"What do you mean?" I asked, gritting my teeth. The doctors had prescribed much stronger pills, but I was managing on fistfuls of ibuprofen. I wasn't about to undo two years of hard-won sobriety just because of a concussion, a laceration, and a few broken bones.

Jonah tapped his fingers against his mouth. "Private nurse. Someone we pay out of pocket."

"That's a fuckload of money." I heard an aggrieved exhale and automatically said, "Sorry mom."

Jonah looked smug, which meant he looked pretty much normal.

"Don't know if you remember a little band called the King Brothers? We *have* a fuckload of money."

My chest tightened. Between my downward spiral after Noelle cheated and the medical bills that were piling up by the second, the "fuckload" of money I'd earned as the guitarist in America's favorite boy band was dwindling fast.

He must have seen the clouded look on my face and instantly waved his hand. "Whatever. I'll pay for it."

"Jonah," I warned.

"Fuck you," he replied amiably. "I'm not making mom have to wash your ass for you for free." He wrinkled his nose and then grinned and slung his arms over her shoulder, completely ignoring her scowl at him for swearing. "Whoever I hire is gonna be properly compensated for that."

It was only my mother's presence in the room that kept me from lifting the middle finger on my uninjured right hand.

The wheels were still turning in Mom's mind. "Sheila Foster's girl is getting her nursing license. She's almost done with the program, I hear," my mom said. "And she's right next door so she'd be available whenever she's not in class."

"So I'll go ask Sheila Foster's girl. Boom. Done." Jonah mimed wiping his hands together.

"Wait, who is Sheila Foster's girl?" I demanded, sitting up as straight as my ribs would allow. "Don't I get a say in this? It's *my* ass that's getting washed, after all."

Jonah leveled his gaze at me. "You have a problem with a pretty neighbor girl playing nursemaid, dude?"

I played along. "She's pretty, huh?" But it wasn't like it mattered. Since Noelle, I'd basically been a monk. In the two years since our breakup, there had only been one girl. The girl I'd danced with the night of my brother's cancelled performance back in December. The girl who'd kissed me like she was drowning and I was her life preserver. The girl I'd thought about every day since that night. But she'd run before I'd gotten her name.

Now her face was a shimmery blur in my wounded brain. All I had of her was a single memory of one lost, perfect kiss.

The fall had jarred the memory loose so that I only had the barest recollection. Like trying to recall a dream. And I knew that was for the best. It wasn't like I was going to try and find her. That kiss belonged to the guy on the video. He died right there, the moment he slammed into the canyon wall. And I was reborn as a useless asshole who has to be waited on by his mother. That girl I kissed would want nothing to do with me. Nothing at all.

Maybe a pretty nursemaid would erase her from my brain. "Fine," I yawned. "She can't be worse than Ana." I leaned back on my pillow, my eyelids suddenly heavy. I opened them exactly once before sleep took hold of me. "Thanks man," I said to my brother.

Chapter Two

EVERLY

I looked down at my Anatomy notes and then back up at my laptop screen. The green "online" light was lit up next to the picture of my sister. In this one she was riding a camel with the pyramids of Giza in the background. I hadn't even known she'd been to Egypt.

I looked back down at my notes. I wasn't sure why I was studying after the news I got this morning. Thanks to some monumental screw-up with the registrar, I'd been taking a class all semester that I had never been fully enrolled in. "No problem," they'd told me. "We'll enroll you now, you just have to pay for the credits. Check or charge?"

When they told me how much it was going to cost, I'd started laughing.

It was the end of the semester. My student loans were exhausted a long time ago. I didn't have three hundred dollars to my name, much less the nearly three thousand they were asking for. But without it, I wasn't going to graduate and no amount of studying was going to change that.

"Desperate times," I muttered. I snapped the notebook shut and in one smooth motion I hit the "call" button before I could psych myself out any further.

The frantic beeping of the Skype connection seemed to be louder than usual. "Fuck," I hissed and turned down the volume on my laptop before glancing up at the ceiling. When there were no noises of stirring from above me, I sighed with relief.

The call picked up and my sister's frozen, smiling face went all fuzzy on my screen before reforming pixel by pixel and the connection solidified mid sentence. "—hear from you again!"

"How are you?" I asked, leaning in a little.

"Stir crazy," she sighed. "They're putting us up in this sketchy hotel in Hanoi. I don't feel like I can leave without an armed guard."

I exhaled. Even when she was complaining about it, Abby's life still sounded more exciting than anything I'd ever dreamed of. "That sucks," was all I could manage to add to that topic.

"How's school?" Abriella asked, fiddling with something offscreen. "You're almost done now, right?"

I swallowed and glanced up at the ceiling again. Were they awake up there? "That's why I called," I said softly.

"What? You have to speak up. This connection is terrible." She went all pixelated again as if to prove her point.

I pressed my lips together. There was the sound of a toilet flushing upstairs. I needed to hurry before they came down. "Abby, I need to borrow some money," I blurted.

My sister's face was frozen on the screen. I took a deep breath, ready to repeat myself when her disembodied voice came out of the speaker. "How much?"

Abby knew why I couldn't ask our parents. My mother still considered both of us traitors for not following her into the family business she "slaved like a dog to build" for us. But while Abriella had at least chosen an exciting and vaguely glamorous career that allowed her to travel the world as an international flight attendant, I'd chosen to, in the words of my mother, "carry pans of shit for a living," and the fact that I'd wanted to be a nurse since I was a child meant nothing to her.

"There was a mix-up at the registrar," I told Abby quickly. There wasn't enough time to go into detail, not with the water running upstairs. "I need twenty nine hundred dollars to be able to graduate on time. Otherwise I can't take my boards."

The picture unfroze and suddenly Abby was leaning in really close. "—wire you the money," she was saying.

"Oh thank god."

"But Everly. One thing."

"Yeah, of course."

"I need it back," she said, blowing out a long exhale. "You know I'm saving every scrap I can for the wedding."

My sister was marrying a pilot. Or at least that was her claim. The engagement period had stretched out to three and a half years now and the wedding date still wasn't set. "When do you need it by?" I said, my throat tightening a little.

"Like in a month," my sister said at the same time my mother's voice rang out from behind me, "There's my globe-trotting girl!"

My mother still smelled like sweat and sugar from the night before. She usually didn't wake from her afternoon nap until dinnertime. The sound of the Skype call connecting must have woken her. "Hi mom," Abby said with an easy smile as my mother shoved her face into the frame.

I swallowed. With my mom here now, there was no way to plead for more time. How was I supposed to pay Abby back in a month? This bought me time to take my boards but I was still right back where I started. Instead of a week, I now needed a month. I still needed money. Fast.

"How are you, honey?" my mom shouted in my ear, but it wasn't me she was talking to. I inhaled sharply and leaned to the left to make space for her, only to bump into my father as he sandwiched me in from the other side. "Where are you now?" he shouted so loudly she didn't need Skype to hear him.

"Hanoi," Abby said. "I fly the Kyoto leg tomorrow. Then a hop to Tokyo before we make the long haul to LA."

"Tokyo! How exciting!" Mom cooed. I could see her maniacally proud grin in the small window up to the right of the screen.

"Watch out for Godzilla!" my dad boomed. He made the same joke every time my sister flew to Japan.

"I will," she said with a long-suffering smile.

"I'm glad you called. I wanted to tell you that they're doing weddings at the lakefront up in Reckless Falls now." My mother was suddenly all business. She wanted this wedding seemingly more than my sister did. "With catering from that new restaurant, Indigo?"

"It's not new, Mom," I murmured, but she ignored me.

"And I was just thinking, what a wonderful venue, you know? So classy and impressive with the water right there, you could—"

"Mom," Abriella sighed. "I can't talk about this right now, okay? I have three hours to shower and sleep before I have to get on a plane again."

"Oh well yes, of course." My mom was instantly deferential. "Make sure you take care of yourself, okay?"

"And watch out for Godzilla!" my Dad added, cracking himself up.

The call ended and my parents stepped back from crowding me. I inhaled sharply and unclenched my fists, absentmindedly rubbing the half moons my fingernails had dug into my palms.

My mom headed to the coffee maker. My dad yawned and leaned over me. Before I realized what he was doing he had grabbed all my carefully arranged notecards and jumbled them into a pile.

"Dad," I said as I grabbed his arm, "I'm studying."

"It's almost dinnertime," my mom called from the corner of the kitchen. My dad nodded and dumped an armload of notebooks and study aids onto the floor by my schoolbag. I blinked slowly and tried to feel outraged but the most I could muster was a sigh.

My parents ate at four in the afternoon and then went back to bed until two in the morning. That was the start of their day as the premier bakery in town. It had always been like this growing up and I hadn't realized how odd it was until I entered the real world and realized that my schedule never matched with the rest of society. I could never have friends over. I could never even really go over to friends' houses because my parents expected me to have dinner at four with them. And on nights when I didn't have a clinical, the expectation was that I'd be home at 9:30pm, "so mom won't worry," according to my dad. I was the only twenty-two year old with a curfew on the planet, I was sure of it.

I sighed again. Then I stood up. I could start a fight and insist they let me finish studying, or I could give in and disappear into my room and allow them to forget I lived here in the first place.

But I was saved from having to make that decision by the sound of the doorbell.

We all froze. Both of my parents were in their bathrobes. "Go see who it is," my mom instructed, tightened the belt of her robe.

I started for the door and then turned back and pointedly closed my laptop before sliding it into my bag.

The doorbell rang again. "Coming!" I shouted, feeling an exasperation that seemed completely out of proportion to the situation, but that was normal for me. I was used to being angry when there was no reason to be. At least I'd learned to hide it now so my mother no longer called me irrational.

I went to the never-used front door and stood on my tiptoes to look out the narrow rectangular window at the top.

Then bounced back down and took an involuntary step back in surprise.

"Who is it?" my mother called from the kitchen.

I slowly rose back up on my toes, convinced I had hallucinated. Then I wondered if I had somehow been sucked back in time to ten years ago and my deepest, dearest twelve-year-old fantasy was inexplicably coming true.

How else to explain Jonah King at my door?

Of course, there was the other, more practical explanation of his family being our neighbors, but my heart wasn't feeling particularly practical to see the same hazel eyes that had looked out from the posters that adorned my bedroom growing up.

"It's Jonah," I said, and tore open the door so fast it banged against the wall.

Jonah King was standing on my porch. Smiling at me. And even though I wasn't a pathetic neighbor girl with a debilitating crush anymore, one look at him had me feeling thirteen again. "Hi Everly," he said in the voice that had launched me into puberty.

Some part of me squealed internally that he knew my name. Then I remembered that yes, once again, his family lived just up the road. We could see their roof from our kitchen and when the sun set, the shadow of it cut across our front lawn. Every day the Kings literally overshadowed us.

His half-self-deprecating, half-self-assured grin was as good as it was at the height of his career, if not better. "I'm glad you're home."

My heart leaped right into my throat and lodged itself there, making it difficult to speak. "Me too," I breathed, before I realized how silly that sounded.

He pretended not to notice the blush that threatened me with spontaneous combustion. He just looked down with those hazel eyes. "You're a nursing student, right?"

I licked my lips. There were a million reasons why Jonah might need to know this, but my mind went right to the dirty ones. I imagined him with his shirt off, asking my professional opinion on whether his muscles could get any bigger.

"I am," I may have said. Whether he heard me or not was debatable, since my voice wasn't working at all anymore.

"Great," he said, rubbing his hands together.

"Well hello there, Jonah." I had an overwhelming urge to shove my mother out of the way as she stepped into my space. "What brings one of our famous neighbors over here?"

Jonah looked at my mom so I did too and oh god, was she actually batting her eyelashes? Every instinct I had told me to back up, to fade into the background, to let her take over, but this was Jonah King here and he was here for *me*. "I've got it, mom," I said tightly.

She looked at me like she'd forgotten I was there. But before she could scoff, Jonah nodded. "I wanted to ask Everly if she needed a job."

"A job?" My heart started racing. A job. Money. I could pay Abby back and still finish my classes and— "What kind of job?"

"Would you mind coming with me?" He glanced at my hovering mother. "I can show you what I'm talking about."

I was already putting on my coat.

"Dinner's almost ready, Everly!" I could hear how irritated my mom was right now but she wanted to seem supportive in front of Jonah. "I'll keep yours warm for you, okay?"

I didn't thank her. I wasn't sure I could trust my voice, walking next to Jonah the way I was. Instead of the bright sunshine and flitting butterflies of my girlish daydreams, there was gray drizzle and depressed looking squirrels, but still, I was walking next to Jonah King. I had to resist the urge to reach for his hand.

He glanced down at me. "You probably heard about Gabe, right?"

I had been studying the way the fine mist of rain clung to his stubble. "Who?"

"My brother," he said, a little sharply.

"Right." I snapped out of the fantasy of Jonah and dove right into the fantasy of Gabe.

Not fantasy. Memory.

But it had only been one night. And he had no idea who I was. Hell, the way I'd behaved that night, *I* had no idea who I was. I didn't kiss guys in the dark like that. That wasn't something a girl like me did.

A guy like Gabriel King, though, he probably kissed like that with girls all the time. So while that night was special to me, he hadn't thought of it since. I was sure of it.

So I bit my lip and nodded. "Right. Gabe." We were out on the road now, crossing the little one-lane bridge over the creek. Above us, the big rambling yellow farmhouse that had been in the King family for four generations rose like part of the landscape. "That was pretty scary, what happened to him."

"He's a fucking idiot," Jonah sighed, somehow managing to make those words sound affectionate. Then he looked down at me with those hazel eyes again. "I need you to do something for me."

I stared back up at him, hypnotized as we walked around the sloped lawn towards the back of the house. "Anything," I breathed and dove right back in to fantasizing about Jonah and what he could possibly want. If he was heading out on tour soon, maybe he needed someone to monitor his health. I could take his vitals while he sat there looking handsome. Shirtless, of course. And of course he would probably need topical creams administered, after his shows, something to stave off the stiffness after he gave it his all onstage. I'd have to make sure to rub it deep into his muscles...

"I need you to be Gabe's nurse."

I stumbled a little. He reached out to grab my arm before I fell just as we pushed our way into the glass-walled sunroom that jutted out of the back of the Kings' house. "Hey asshole!" Jonah crowed. "I found someone to wipe your ass!"

There was a huge hospital bed sitting dead center in the middle of the sunroom. The wavering light that filtered through the raindrops on the glass walls gave everything a mottled, underwater look, as if I was walking through a dream.

The man propped up in the bed looked like he was doing some dreaming too. "Shit," Jonah hissed. "He's asleep."

"No need to wake him," I said quickly. I knew Gabe had been hurt badly. It was all the town could talk about these last few weeks. How he'd survived a BASE jumping accident—which was a miracle, the ladies at my mom's church attested—but was looking down the road of a long, arduous rehab, his daredevil days over.

But I hadn't known just how *different* he would look.

My memory of Gabe King was hazy and rum-soaked for sure, but it was still a jolt to see him like this. His eyes were at half mast, lids heavy from what I assumed was a massive dose of painkillers. His sandy hair—lighter than his brother's—was long and in desperate need of a trim, an untamed tangle that fell down along his bearded jaw. Underneath his hospital gown, I could see the dark outlines of tattoos across his rangey muscles that were somehow un-atrophied from weeks in a hospital bed. But even confined to a bed with his side bandaged and both ankles encased in booted casts, he still looked wild. Like the kind of guy who would pull a girl to him and slide his hands down to...

"Fuck," Gabe hissed, his eyelids fluttering.

I held my breath as those hazel eyes met mine and smiled tentatively. "Hi again." My heart was in my throat.

He blinked and then yawned. "Who're you?" he mumbled.

Then fell back to sleep.

I licked my lips. Clearly he didn't remember me at all. I stood there, feeling empty and blank for a long moment, surprised at myself for feeling surprised. He didn't remember. That was a good thing, I told myself. That meant it wouldn't be weird.

I still really needed the money, anyway. So I tamped down the competing emotions, looked up to Jonah, and smiled blandly. "When can I start?"

Chapter Three

EVERLY

Someone in the past twenty years had painted my car a matte black. The paint job and the lingering specter of death that hung around it all the time led me to name it The Grim Reaper, which made my dad upset since it had been his car, then my sister's. But it was mine now. A boxy 1997 Chevy station wagon. It even looked like a hearse.

"Come on, baby," I begged as it choked and sputtered. I had this complicated ritual to get old Grimmy started. "Come on," I cooed, tapping the accelerator halfway down three times before flicking into neutral at the same time I turned the key.

My classmate, when she saw this ridiculous dance I performed every time I started my car, had laughed and rolled her eyes, but it hadn't failed me, until now.

"Fuck you, come on," I whined. But Grim sensed fear. You had to have a firm hand, and a calm heart. He could look deep inside of you like some oracle of your purest intentions. Sometimes he decided you just didn't really need to run to the grocery store.

Thankfully, this morning Grim smiled upon me and deemed my need to leave worthy enough to choke to life. I revved his engine precisely two more times to make sure he wasn't joking around with me, then pulled out of the driveway.

After the triumph of getting Grim started, it almost seemed criminal that I had to turn him off again so soon. I pulled into the Kings' driveway and contemplated leaving him running, but I couldn't afford the gas. Not until I got my first King-sized paycheck.

I stopped and grinned to myself as I headed to the back door of the Kings' house. That was a good one, but there weren't many people who shared my love of a good pun. My friends online might, but no one in person. I'd have to remember it and tell it to Abby next time I talked to her. Which might not be for another few weeks.

I entered through the back door. Mrs. King had given me a key, and Duke, their old dog, only raised his head a curious inch before flopping back down again. "Some watchdog," I snorted. Then I looked around. "Gabe?" I called. "It's Everly. You ready?"

I had only ever been inside the King house when there were people all around. They'd always thrown barbecues when the boys got home from a tour—even in the dead of winter—and as their neighbors we had an open invitation. But the house had always been full of noise and the clatter of people as curious as I was about the brothers and our town's claim to fame. I'd never been in here when it was silent.

Mrs. King had held her job as a part-time library clerk since before I was born, gamely smiling and answering questions about her sons before directing people to the non-fiction section. That's where she was now. And I knew that Mr. King helped out at Andolino's Garage whenever they had a particularly finicky car come through. Claire worked for a developer in Reckless Falls, I knew that. But I had no idea where Finn, or Beau or, yeah, Jonah might be. I hadn't expected to be alone when I came by to pick up Gabe and take him to his physical therapy appointment. I had to trust that one of them had told him I was coming in the first place.

The silence was thick. I felt strangely like a prowler and had to resist the urge to turn around and head right back out of the door again.

"Gabe?" I called, more forcefully now. I poked my head into the living room, stepping around the inert, snoring Labrador that lay like a rug in the middle of the room. Back in the sunroom, I could see the sheets were thrown back on the empty hospital bed. I'd have to change those when I got back.

"Gabe?" I said again, spinning in a slow circle in the center of the living room. The house was so quiet I could only hear little sounds. Background noises. The muffled tick of a clock somewhere. The whoosh of the heat in the vents. The faint patter of rain on the windows.

And from above me, a thump and a muffled cry.

I was running even before I registered where the sound was coming from. I took the stairs two at a time, landing in the unfamiliar upstairs. "Hello?" I called, throwing open each door in turn. Empty bedrooms and overstuffed closets were all I could find until I threw open the last door in the hallway.

It thudded into something hard and unyielding.

"Motherfucker!" Gabe cried.

The hard and unyielding object had been his head.

I clapped my hand to my mouth, dropped down to a crouch, and reached through the gap to the other side of the door. "Shit, did you fall?" I worried, reaching out and trying to find a pulse at his neck out of instinct.

He batted my hand away with an angry growl. "Who the hell are you? What are you fucking—ow!" he cried again as I tried to slide into the bathroom, only to thump the corner of the door into his head again.

"It's okay," I reassured him. "I'm your nurse and—"

I slid all the way into the bathroom and trailed off, my words dying in my throat.

There, sprawled flat across the bathroom floor, was all six feet and many extra inches of naked and vulnerable yet still strangely frightening Gabe King. Scars and tattoos decorated his torso like a roadmap, twining in a network of pathways leading down to...

I tried to jump back but my heel hit something and I sat down heavily—

On the open toilet.

"Fuck!" I cried, leaping back up again. I was too late. My ass now sported a perfect "o" of toilet water.

"Ow!" Gabe grimaced as I jostled into him. "What the fuck?"

"Sorry," I said. "Lost my balance." I did not tell him that the sight of his cock had made me literally fall over. I was a nurse. Cocks shouldn't get me flustered. I took a deep breath and looked at it again to desensitize myself and promptly got doubly flustered. "Were you bathing alone?" I demanded, trying to mask my agitation with irritation. The toilet water was gradually seeping into my underwear. Thank god it had been flushed. "What the hell were you thinking?"

He grimaced and hauled himself up onto his good elbow, then pinned me with eyes that were way too green and familiar. "I was thinking," he said, through gritted teeth, "that my brother hired a nurse from next door to pick me up for PT and I didn't want to smell like a wet gym sock when she arrived. Guess it's my good breeding and all," he said pointedly. "You mind grabbing me a fucking towel?" he asked as I wrested my eyes away from his fairly impressive penis once more.

"Oh, yeah." Some fucking professional I was. Burning up with shame, I grabbed a fluffy towel from the rack and draped it over his groin. He let out a sigh of either relief or exasperation, I couldn't tell, and pushed himself higher on his elbow. "Here, I'll help you."

"Please," he scoffed, waving me away.

"You have two broken ankles and five broken ribs," I reminded him. "Let me get behind you."

"You can't lift me. Look at you."

"I'm five foot nine."

"And a hundred pounds soaking wet."

I was a sturdy one hundred and sixty pounds and I'd thrown shot-put in high school. "You'd make a terrible guess-my-weight guy at the county fair," I chuckled. "Stick with your day job." I wedged myself between the door and his head. "Lift your head for me?"

"You're not going to be able to lift me."

"How about you shut up and let me try?"

He twisted his head to look at me. "You say you're my nurse? Thought they were supposed to have nice bedside manners and shit."

"I'm not actually a full-fledged nurse yet," I snapped. And then I slipped my arms under his back and hauled stubborn, naked Gabe King to his feet.

Chapter Four

GABE

She lifted me.

This random pissed off chick—who kept staring at my accidentally exposed cock like it had offended her—just wrestled all two-hundred and twenty pounds of me upright without the slightest grunt of exertion.

It was humiliating. It was emasculating. It was...

Fucking impressive.

She twisted me and turned me and at the last minute slammed the toilet closed before depositing me right down on the lid. "Now, where are your crutches?" she asked. "All the way over here? You were trying to reach them when you fell, weren't you? You're lucky they didn't land on your head."

"I'm sorry, but..." I said, staring at this girl who'd appeared out of nowhere—like some kind of blue-eyed, body-building guardian angel—right when I'd lost my fucking balance in the shower like the old lady on a Life Alert commercial. I'd literally fallen and couldn't get up. "I should know you, right?"

"Everly," she said, in this resigned tone of voice. Like she was used to reminding people about who she was. "From next door."

Everly. The name conjured up flashes of wide eyes under a heavy fringe of bangs. A solemn, staring girl in unfashionable hand-me-downs standing on the other side of the creek while my siblings and I played in the backyard. Watching but never joining in.

Those memories didn't jibe with the blonde badass currently invading my personal space while I sat naked on a toilet. "So you're my nurse now?"

"I'm studying to be an RN," she said with stiff pride. "I take my boards in a couple weeks."

The humidity in the bathroom was making little hairs fuzz up from her tight ponytail, haloing her in blonde. She had full cheeks and full lips that gave the impression of softness but her eyes were cold blue steel. There was something about them that made the back of my brain tickle. I'd seen her before, of that I was certain, but then again, of course I had, she was the neighbor girl after all.

As if she could tell I was studying her, she stared right back. Openly, without even trying to sneak glances or be subtle about it. There was something about how direct her gaze was that made my skin heat up in a way that had nothing to do with the lingering heat of the shower. My cock stirred as if it liked the attention. "Um," I said, angry at how vulnerable I was right now, "that's cool and all, but can I have my crutches now?"

"No."

"Are you trying to hold me hostage or something?"

"No." She rolled her eyes. "First I need to check your vitals."

"I'm naked."

"I'm a nurse," she huffed. "You think yours is the first naked body I've ever seen?" I couldn't tell if it was the heat in here that was coloring her cheeks or if it was something else.

She leaned forward and stared into my eyes for a moment, then grabbed my wrist. I held my breath as she pressed two fingers to the pulse I was inexplicably hearing in my ears. I willed my cock to stay where it was and not enjoy the feel of her fingers on my skin so damn much.

After what seemed like an eternity, she stepped back with a nod. "Now, do you remember what you were doing before you fell?"

I blinked at her. I'd traveled the world and had crowds screaming my name. I'd had my own TV show with ratings good enough to warrant talk of a new season. But this chick didn't seem impressed by any of that and I was surprised at how annoyed that made me. She was all business and seemed bound and determined to ignore my naked discomfort. "Getting out of the tub because I heard someone prowling around downstairs," I snarked. "Somebody who showed up a lot earlier than she needed to."

She didn't take the bait. "Mm hmm, and tell me what happened just after you fell?"

I tightened the towel around my waist. "My nurse slammed a door into my head."

"Okay and do you remember why I'm here?" she asked.

"You mean other than to give me the third degree?"

"I'm checking for a concussion," she said primly. "Making sure you're not confused about recent events."

"Oh, recent events are pretty damn confusing, I'll tell you that much. But no, I remember you're supposed to take me to my first PT appointment." I reached out. "And in order to get to it, I'm going to need my crutches so I can go get dressed."

"No way I'm letting you dress yourself," she said. "You need assistance, especially with lifting your arms over your head. How many ribs did you break again?" But she handed me my crutches.

I grimaced, scrabbling with one hand to keep the towel wrapped around my waist while trying to maneuver around her with the other. The towel fell again. "Fuck it," I growled. "Mine isn't the first naked body you've seen, right?"

"Nope," she said, her scowl deepening. "Now, where are your clothes? Don't tell me you have to come all the way up here to get dressed. Why are you even on the second floor, anyway?"

"This is where the shower is," I said, hauling myself as fast as I could to my old bedroom.

But she was right on my heels, scolding me like some kind of human blue jay. I swung myself into the doorway and reached out.

"Hey!" she cried as I shut the door in her face. "What the hell are you doing?"

"Getting dressed in private?" I answered, hobbling over to my bed and taking a deep, panicked breath.

Plenty of chicks had seen me naked since I broke up with Noelle. But every single one of them had been too busy trying to save my life to give a shit about how I looked in the nude.

Everly-from-next-door should have felt the same way. She was another nurse, after all. But for some reason it mattered to me this time. It mattered that she saw me, scarred and crippled, weak and so out of shape that little hobbled sprint down the hallway had me feeling out of breath.

I gritted my teeth as the crutches dug into my armpits. My ankles were screaming from the slight weight I was putting on them now.

I'd swung my legs out at the last minute. Which saved me from slamming my head into the rock face and scrambling my brains like an egg, but left me with two shattered ankles. Pins and screws were holding them together now, and I swore I could feel those bits of metal grinding around in there. I'd just finished washing myself but the pain was already making cold sweat prickle at my hairline. I looked down at the side of my old bed.

The two big Frankenstein boots were sitting there, staring me down like a guilty conscience. I'd graduated from plaster casts that couldn't get wet to these monstrosities, but at least I could take them off. The bath Everly had interrupted had been the first time I'd been alone in the bathroom in months. It was pathetic how good it felt to have some privacy and some fucking dignity and...

I heard a decidedly unfeminine curse out in the hallway. The door slammed open.

I snapped my head up and stared at the red-faced Everly in open disbelief. "What the fuck are you doing?" I demanded, yanking the covers off the bed and holding them against my over-exposed dick.

The expression on her face reminded me of the one my dog made when he stopped being gentle playing tug-of-war and started growling and yanking. "You're my patient, which means you're my responsibility," she said, planting her hands on her hips. "There's no way in hell I'm letting you get dressed and risk falling again on my watch." The way she said “my watch” landed like a sack of guilty bricks against my chest.

I held up my good hand. “Seriously, Everly. I don’t need...”

“Sit,” she barked.

For some reason, I sat.

She nodded. “Let’s find you some clothes.” She started yanking open drawers. “Here you go.”

“That’s my brother’s shirt,” I said. She was pretty but she was really starting to piss me off.

She rolled her eyes. “Who cares?”

“Me?”

“Fine.” She rummaged around some more. “How about this?”

I threw up my good hand in surrender. “I haven’t worn that in ten years and I told my mother to throw it out, but whatever.” I shrugged. “Give it here.”

She nodded, but she didn’t hand it over. Instead she stalked over to the side of the bed and stood in front of me.

I looked up at her from where I was sitting and took in the determined set of her mouth and the little worried furrow between her eyebrows. She seemed to be scrutinizing me as closely as I was her and for a moment we just looked at each other in complete silence. Again I had that tickle in the back of my brain.

Noelle was a chatterer. She liked to fill my ears with her every thought, a never-ending flood of words that sometimes threatened to drown me. In the years since I’d ended it, I wondered more than once if she hadn’t kept talking in order to keep me from thinking. Because maybe, if I had a chance to catch my breath, I might have realized what she was up to behind my back.

Everly was obviously not a chatterbox, so I just stared back at her. It was like a weird game of silent chicken. Whoever talks first, loses.

Finally she exhaled. “Lift your arms,” she said, holding the shirt over my head.

My brief triumph over winning the standoff was overthrown the second I tried to do what she asked me. I lifted my arms and grimaced. “That’s as far as I can go.”

Her soft mouth screwed down into a frown. "When's the last time you took your painkillers?"

"I didn't." I raised my chin defiantly.

"What?"

"I'm not taking them."

"Are you insane?"

"Some people think so, yeah," I said.

She shook her head. "So you're taking nothing for the pain of five broken ribs, a laceration, and two broken ankles?"

"Ibuprofen."

"That's like bringing a knife to a gun fight."

"It's fine."

"Why are you being so stubborn?"

I glanced up at her. She'd grown up next door to us but I was only noticing her for the first time. I wondered if the feeling was mutual. Being in the public eye meant it was close to impossible to know how much information anyone had about you. Had they heard of you? Were they obsessive fans or completely clueless? Or were they haters who spent time on web forums typing in ALL CAPS about how you ate babies for sport? You knew nothing about them but they thought they knew everything about you.

Did she have any knowledge of what had gone on in my life these past few years? Did she know about my break-up with Noelle St. Lucia, the breakup of the band, my stint in rehab? My slow climb back into relevancy with a cheesy-ass reality show where I went around the world doing extreme sports?

She knew about my accident, that much was clear, but as far as I could tell, she didn't know anything else about me.

And to my surprise I found that suited me just fine.

Instead of explaining my stubbornness when it came to painkillers, I just smiled. "I'm a stubborn guy."

She rolled her eyes. "I'm noticing this," she said as she slid my shirt over my head.

She disappeared from my view for a moment, and then reappeared even closer when my head popped out of the collar. She was so close I could feel heat rising from her skin and see each one of those fine blonde baby hairs that haloed her face. As she bent to help me into my boxers, the collar of her uniform fell away, revealing the strong slope of her shoulder and a bright pink bra strap that made me sit up a little straighter.

In the process of dressing me, her hands must have touched every inch of my skin, and as they did, the strangest thing was happening. Her feathery touch drew trails along my skin that alternately cooled and burned. Goosebumps broke out on my arms.

Of course she noticed. "Are you feeling feverish? I think I need to check your vitals again. That fall was pretty spectacular."

I clenched my teeth. The pain in my ankles was searing and my tentative hold on civility was starting to fray. The couple sessions with the physical therapist in the hospital had left me gasping and shaking and pretty fucking close to tears. And now I was supposed to go do all of that again, but this time with Everly there watching everything with those steely blue eyes. Watching me struggle.

So far this girl had seen me naked, hurt, embarrassed, and vulnerable.

Enough was enough.

I crossed my arms in front of my chest and willed the last remaining bits of my dignity to assert themselves. "Yeah, it was pretty bad," I said, lifting my chin. "Maybe I had better not go today." I shifted until I was lying back on the bed. "I'll call and cancel the appointment. Why don't you head home?"

And that's where I made my first mistake.

Ana, my last nurse, was always ready to be let out early. It required little more than a, "I think everything's fine," to get her out of my hair. I figured the same bullshit would apply to Everly, who, after all, had other shit going on right now. I figured she'd jump at the chance to knock off early.

When the steel in her eyes hardened to diamonds, I realized I'd figured completely wrong.

Chapter Five

GABE

Everly opened the door and turned to glare at me.

I bit the inside of my cheek and maneuvered myself clumsily through the door, then hobbled to the nearest chair and plopped down to glare back at her. “There,” I said. “I’m here. You win.”

She eyed me for a second, then went over to check us in with the receptionist. I took the moment to exhale a long breath.

My ankles were definitely hurting, but worse was the pain in my side. After weeks of lying in a bed, I was breathless after the slightest exertion, but my newly healed ribs weren’t quite up to the strain I was putting on them. The ride over here hadn’t exactly helped my elevated breathing rate either.

Everly came and sat next to me, perched at the edge of the seat like she was ready to leap away at any second. “I’d be jumpy too,” I told her. “If that was my car.”

Luckily this time I had figured her correctly. She turned with an evil grin. “Are you talking smack about The Grim Reaper?”

Her boxy, black monstrosity was a Frankenstein’s monster of cobbled together parts. It had been patched and painted over so many times I could barely tell the make and model anymore, in spite of the gearhead tendencies my father had nurtured in us. "Your car mutated," I said. "How old is that thing?"

"I'm the fourth owner."

"So it's an heirloom?"

She snorted. "It's a piece of shit and I hate it," she sighed, reaching back to smooth her ponytail. "But it's what I'm stuck with at the moment."

"Not gonna lie, I thought we were going to stall out there a few times."

"Don't worry about it," she said, waving her hand dismissively. "I know how to handle The Grim."

She sure as fuck did. Just like how she'd lifted me with no apparent strain, she'd also weathered the kicking, bucking, knocking engine like a complete pro. I was pretty sure she kept the car running through sheer force of will.

And for the second time today, I found myself impressed with this odd, surly girl that had somehow escaped my notice until right now.

The door opened. "King?" called a therapist standing by the door.

Everly leaped to her feet and set to laying out my crutches. I grunted, embarrassed, but I secretly appreciated the help. "Ready?" she asked me.

"No," I admitted. "Can you wait out here maybe?"

"Nope," she replied, but she said it with a grin.

I rolled my eyes, started towards the door, and then froze.

Icewater poured into my veins in one breath and then in the next I was burning with rage.

"You okay?" Everly asked softly. She'd seen me stop short. "You need help?"

I shook my head and willed my fists to unclench. Because now that I was closer, I could see the therapist only looked like Noelle. Same big blue eyes, wide and deceptively innocent. But her mouth was different, wider with thinner lips.

She wasn't Noelle.

She wasn't Noelle.

The memory came only in flashes now. Pictures, like snapshots in time. Noelle leaping to her feet. My manager's smile as he zipped up his jeans.

The rose-gold engagement ring bouncing a little when it fell from my hand.

"Gabe?" Everly hissed. She slid her arm through mine. "Hey, Gabe?"

I took a deep, steadying breath. The therapist gave me a bright, confused smile and held out her hand. "I'm Kristyn," she said, in a low, throaty voice that sounded nothing like Noelle's.

Because she wasn't Noelle.

"This is Gabriel King," Everly piped up. She tugged a little on my arm and I felt myself being propelled forward. She had my arm tight in hers, and it felt good to lean on her. Just a little. She was solid and strong, but her fingers were long and delicate and the way they curled around my bicep was doing a lot to push the memory of my ex out of my brain. "And I'm his nurse, Everly Foster."

"Beverly?"

Everly grimaced. "No B," she said tightly. "Gabe is here for his first appointment."

"What she said," I grumbled as Everly let go of me so I could fit through the door. My arm felt cold without her holding it.

Kristyn shut the door behind her. "Have a seat," she said, gesturing to the padded table nearest us.

I looked around. The place was bigger than I had expected. It looked like a cross between a workout gym and a massage parlor. A tinny, staticky radio played in the corner and I had to chuckle when I heard the song that was playing through the busted speakers. "Seriously?"

"I used to love this song," Kristyn said casually as Jonah's voice warbled through the space. My fingers still made the shapes of the guitar chords out of habit but at least I didn't bust out with my harmonies out of some perverted reflex. My voice was probably shit by now anyway. I hadn't played music since we broke the band up. "Is it weird?" Kristyn asked. "Being back home again after..." she gestured to the radio where my brothers and I shout-sang about *dynamite kisses going one two three boom*. "After all that?"

All while she was busily paging through my chart, her eyes were firmly on me and I wondered if she still had her laminated "Princess Sisters: The Official Fan Club of the King Brothers" card in her wallet.

"Which one was your favorite?" Everly interjected before I could answer. She shot me another one of her evil grins.

Kristyn gave me a guilty look. "Beau," she mumbled quickly. "He's so sensitive."

"He's got a big lumberjack beard now," I told her. "Looks like a woodsman."

She shook her head a little and laughed. "No way," she said, clinging to her perception of poetic Beau, The Quiet One.

"I liked Jonah," Everly said.

"You and everyone else," I muttered.

"He was always too arrogant for me," Kristyn said, shaking her head.

I cleared my throat. "Me too," I said, with a sigh.

She laughed. "Well, shall we get started then?"

I looked between her and Everly. "Sure, I mean, unless you two wanted to do some more gossiping about my brothers while I waited."

Everly just laughed, but Kristyn reddened noticeably and jumped over to stand next to me. "Slide off the table for me?"

I glared at her, but dutifully followed instructions, leaning heavily on my crutches.

"Right, and let's just..." She took the crutches from me. One and then the other.

And for the first time in three months, I stood under my own power.

Each heartbeat was as loud as a church bell in my head. My nerves jangled. But out of the corner of my eye, I could see Everly watching me closely and that was the only reason I didn't sit back down again. After that debacle in the bathroom, I wanted her to see me standing. I wanted to impress her for reasons I didn't fully understand.

So I gritted my teeth and gave Everly a smile.

She sat up a little straighter. That was it. But it was enough to make me want to see what other kinds of reactions I could pull from her.

I exhaled sharply. "How does that feel?" Kristyn asked. I'd almost forgotten she was there, but she was right at my side, a faint smile twitching around her lips. I wondered if she got off on watching big guys like me sweat it out through the pain. "You're all hunched. Try standing straighter, please."

Straightening up was torture. My ribs twanged like guitar strings, reminding me that I was still at their mercy whenever they might feel like stealing my breath. Inside of my ankles, it felt seriously unstable, like one stiff breeze could knock me down. "I feel like I'm sliding around in there," I said, gesturing downward. I kept my voice low so Everly couldn't hear me complain.

Kristyn nodded like this made a damn bit of sense. "Your muscles have atrophied from weeks of lying down," she said in a normal volume. I glanced in Everly's direction and wished like hell Kristyn would keep her voice down. "We've gotta get your strength back up again."

"Yeah," I said. If I said anything more than that, my voice would betray me. Show how fucked up in the head I was feeling about maybe never walking properly again.

"I want to watch your gait, so follow me. Over here, please." I shuffled like an old man behind her until we reached some weighted contraption. "You've definitely got some work to do with balance but for now we need to get your strength up."

"Yeah, no shit," I hissed.

"Right, so go ahead and put your feet right here," she said, gesturing to a black footpad.

"Uh huh." It looked like a stability ball but it was square instead of round. I glanced at her. "What happens now?"

There was a smile playing around her lips as she looped a rubbery piece of fabric—a stability band like those I recognized from Noelle's Pilates obsession—underneath my foot and handed me the two ends. She looked at me, eyes gleaming.

She was enjoying this.

"Pull up," the manicured sadist smiled.

I tugged on the ends and a strangled cry tore out of my throat. "Slow down!" Everly barked before Kristyn could say a word. "Don't overdo it!"

My whole body was soaked with sweat and I was panting with exertion. Fucking pathetic.

"Try again," Kristyn said lightly.

But her voice was fading from my ears as I looked over at my nurse. Everly was watching, her big round eyes taking in how badly I was failing right now. Her hair was starting to dry from the rain and fuzz back up into a little halo of baby curls around her face. When she caught me looking, she pressed her lips together. Whether it was pity or disapproval, I hated it. I didn't want her looking at me like that. She'd hauled me to my feet like I weighed nothing. This was fucking humiliating.

I gritted my teeth and coaxed ten reps out of one ankle, then ten out of the other out of sheer force of ego. Then I glanced at Everly again.

Was that a ghost of a smile on her lips? I lifted my chin at her and gave another grin. "Maybe next I'll try dressing myself?"

"Don't get ahead of yourself now," my nurse called.

"Right. I don't want to deprive you of the opportunity to stare at my body again."

She reddened, which gave me enough strength to do five more reps on each side.

Over the next hour, Kristyn guided me through a series of exercises so minute they felt like they should barely register. By the end, I was ready to cry out for mercy.

But Everly was watching, so that wasn't happening.

"Okay, last bit!" Kristyn cried. "Let's do ten steps unassisted. Can you try that for me?"

"No problem," I told her. "As long as you don't make me use the band again."

I straightened back up. "Like this now. Short steps. Keep your center of gravity over your front foot."

I looked up at Everly. She was watching me, her lips pressed together. Her expression had slowly morphed over the past hour from irritation to attention.

"Got it," I said. Everly nodded a little like she got it too.

"Ten steps," Kristyn repeated. "Ready and...one!"

Without the boot on, I felt like I was sliding around inside of my own skin. But I stepped forward, mimicking her mincing gait. "Slow down," she instructed. "You don't want to overdo it."

"You just told me to do more," I reminded her, taking another step, then another. I was doing it. Laughing, I took another step, the rush of triumph making my blood sparkle.

"Gabe!" Everly said sharply, leaping to her feet.

"What?" I looked up at her tense face. "I'm just walking. How can I get hurt by walking?" I laughed, feeling the adrenaline spike higher.

It had been ages since I'd felt this, the excitement of sitting just on the edge of too much to handle. The power that came from pushing through my body's self-preservation and fucking going for it. Even if it was something as tiny and unimpressive as walking again, it was still a fucking rush. "Ha!" I shouted as I sprang forward, sweat dampening my brow. "See that? You fucking see that?" Everly was watching me. I took five more steps, faster and faster until, whooping loudly, I half-hugged, half fell against her.

She stumbled back but caught herself, her arms reflexively wrapping around me to keep us both from tumbling to the floor. Hands grabbed and clung as we regained our balance and I slowly realized I had her clutched tightly in my arms.

"I did it," I panted, my cheek pressed against her hair. I could smell rainwater and shampoo and something sweet and subtle that had me inhaling again and again. Her hair was so soft. "I did it," I repeated, my voice a little tighter.

She tilted her head and I felt her hand brush up my back. Her fingers pressed in ever so lightly against my back and that maddening brain tickle made me look down at her again. She looked up at me.

I had my balance again, and I didn't need her help to stand, but all of a sudden, I didn't want to let go.

Chapter Six

EVERLY

There was something in his voice. I didn't think I was imagining it.

He was remembering me now.

He had to be.

I was remembering too. It was all right there, like it was happening again. Without my permission, my hand went sliding up his back. Heat was rising off his skin from his exertion and his scent was everywhere. Under my fingers, the muscles in his back coiled and stretched. My brain was short-circuiting as I traced those muscles so defined he was like a living anatomy textbook. *Latissimus dorsi,* I mentally recited. *Levator scapulae, splenius capitis.* I found myself wondering hysterically if he could help me study for my boards this way.

"You're okay now," I whispered to him. I wasn't sure why I was whispering other than it felt right. "You can stand on your own."

But he didn't move. And neither did I. We stayed there in this strange embrace that made the impersonal space of the therapy room seem completely intimate. All we needed was for the lights to go out and it would be like that night again.

Though his hands were still, a kind of radiation spiraled off them. I could feel his touch in places his hands had never been, raising goosebumps on my skin in twining trails all through my body.

If presented with these symptoms by a patient I would start treating for a fever, but I felt completely healthy. I felt more than healthy, I felt...

Fucking wonderful.

He inhaled again and I felt his chest hitch, hold, and then relax again as he exhaled. Like he was about to say something, but thought better of it. I waited for him to realize he could stand on his own and let go of me, even though I didn't actually want him to. I waited for him to mention the kiss.

Instead he pulled me ever so slightly closer. My leg brushed against his and I was acutely aware of heat gathering in my belly as my head spun dizzily.

Presented with these symptoms, I would start treating for sunstroke. *Administer clear liquids. Apply a cold compress to back of neck...*

Gabe's lip brushed down and I felt his breath against my ear, which made me shiver. *For hypothermia, warm the body's core temperature slowly.*

"I remember you," he said.

All of my studying flew out of my head and I couldn't think of anything but the way his breath tickled my neck. "Everly Foster. From next door."

He chuckled, a low and thrilling sound that made my toes dig into my shoes. "You probably thought I didn't remember you, but I do."

I opened my mouth, and then closed it. Then blinked as warmth traveled up from my belly and right up to the space behind my eyes. Shit. I was not going to cry. Why the fuck did I feel like I wanted to cry? *For panic attacks encourage the patient to take slow, deep breaths...*

I pulled back and looked at him. His arms tightened like he wasn't ready to let me go. I had the strangest feeling of surreality, like I'd stepped into someone else's life. Someone interesting. Someone far more fascinating than boring old me. The way he was looking at me now had me wondering if this was all a delusion and I was about to wake up and find that I'd fallen and hit my head.

"Right," he said, nodding. "You'd come over with your parents to those barbecues my parents always had, right? And you have a sister too, don't you?"

My lips were still parted, the "yes" still on my tongue. I stared at him and swallowed it back down before I could blurt out what I thought he was going to say. My stomach twisted and I felt nauseous. And once again an anger I had no business feeling took hold of me, making my heart start racing. I settled my hand on his arm and gently untangled myself from his embrace.

"I remember you too!" Kristyn piped up. She appeared at our side and I realized that while it had felt like a lifetime standing there wrapped in Gabe's arms, in reality it had only been a few seconds at best. She was holding Gabe's crutches for him, but she was looking at me. "Your sister was in my class!" she burst out. "We were lab partners! Oh my god, how is Abby doing? I hear she's like traveling the world now, right?" She shook her head like we all were the best of friends. "I thought your name sounded familiar!" She screwed up her nose. "But you said Everly, right? Why do I remember it being Beverly?"

For nausea, first determine if the patient has consumed anything poisonous that would require a trip to the emergency department.

I pulled back from Gabe, taking the crutches from Kristyn and shoving them at him in one smooth motion. "It's Everly," I told Kristyn, already a million miles away from this conversation. "Common mistake." I looked at Gabe. "Ready to go? I'll grab your coat."

His tongue flicked out to wet his lips. He was looking at me as if something had him completely confused.

But Kristyn was still stuck on her trip down memory lane. "Funny," she mused. "I must have gone over to Abriella's house a million times, but I never remember seeing you." She looked up from her chart at me with a big smile on her face. "Did you hide in your room a lot?"

I pressed my lips together. Abriella had a zillion friends, all of them blonde and perfect like Kristyn. Petite, pretty girls who understood social rules on a level I never could. When I was younger I used to hang out on the landing and watch them through the banister, trying to decode the mysteries of their popularity, but one afternoon Abby caught me spying on her and threatened to tell mom I was being weird again. So I never spied again.

I also never managed to learn the rules either. "I don't know," I said, shoving Gabe's coat at him. "Maybe."

Kristyn turned her mouth down in an exaggerated frown. "Weird. It's like... you weren't even there." She looked at me for a moment while I held my breath. It felt like my feet were nailed to the floor.

Then she smiled and shook her head. "Well, tell Abby I said hello, okay? Next time she's in town I want to hear all about her adventures."

"Sure," I said. I didn't look at her. I didn't look at Gabe. I kept my eyes in front of me the whole ride home, so I didn't notice how many people just plain didn't notice me at all.

Chapter Seven

GABE

First the voices were muffled, like I was hearing them underwater. I swam upward as they got louder and more distinct. "Wake him up? Is he okay? Ha, he's drooling, you see that?"

Slowly I opened my eyes. The sunroom swam back into focus. As did four faces peering over my bed.

My sister Claire was hovering over my left elbow with that bossy-baby-sister expression on her face. Next to her stood my youngest brother Finn, looking like he was about to crack up laughing at any moment. Which I guess was better than his usual quick-to-take-offense scowl. At the foot of the bed loomed Finn's twin, the older by five minutes Beau. His worried expression was nearly masked by all the freaking hair he'd recently started to let grow on his face.

And then there was my older brother Jonah near my right hand. Although given how he'd been acting lately, I was surprised to see him there rather than up my ass like he usually was. "What do you all want?" I croaked at my siblings.

"Jesus, there you are," Claire complained. "You've been asleep for four straight hours. I was worried one of us was going to have to wake you up."

"We drew straws," Finn added. "None of us wanted to be the one to get punched in the face."

"I don't have the range of motion to punch anyone in the face," I sighed as I rolled over. I was stiff and sore all over. "Fuck."

Jonah looked worried. "You okay?"

I winced as I pushed myself higher in the bed. "PT was a bitch," I explained through gritted teeth. I was sore in places I didn't know it was possible to be sore. A far cry from how I'd felt at the actual appointment.

I remembered how good I'd felt walking for the first time. How high and triumphant. In a fit of celebration, I'd hugged Everly and for a second she seemed into it, but then something made her shut down. I rubbed my good hand down my face. "Fuck," I said again.

"You need water?" Beau asked.

"You his nurse?" Finn teased.

"Fuck off," he sighed, pulling a glass of water out of nowhere and handing it to Jonah who handed it to me.

"Thanks man." I took a drink and winced again.

Both Beau and Jonah saw it. "You take anything?" my older brother asked.

I thought for moment. "Not since this morning."

"I still think you're making this much harder than it needs to be," Jonah said, unable to keep the pompous-know-it-all out of his voice for too long. "Taking something for the pain in your body is much different than..."

"Taking something for the pain in my mind?" I finished.

My three brothers looked at each other in turn. Claire stared at a point in the middle distance. There was the telltale sound of shuffling feet.

This was exasperating. I shook my head. "No, it's got the same effect on my fucked-up brain. I don't *want* to need anything."

"It's not the same!" Jonah protested, but Beau shot him a look and Beau was probably the only person in the world besides his fiancée Ruby who could get Jonah to shut the fuck up for once.

I handed him the glass and let my head fall back on the pillow.

"You've any idea how hard I had to work to get sober?" I said through gritted teeth. I glanced at my elder brother. "No, you don't."

Jonah winced, and I could feel the guilt rolling off of him in waves. Maybe he was still trying to make up for the fact that he hadn't been around, that we'd gone nearly two years without speaking, without clearing the air after the breakup both of our band and my relationship with Noelle. He'd spent the last two years hell bent on proving he could make it without us, only to realize recently that he wanted us again. Wanted to be brothers once more.

That's why, as near as I could tell, he spent so much time hovering around here, up my ass so far I needed a crowbar to get him loose.

I'd told him we were cool half a million times at this point. But it was clear he didn't believe me. And hell, I probably didn't help things with the way I acted. The rage I'd felt towards him still came back every so often. The need to needle him about Bennett was still there. Even though I fought it, sometimes I lost.

"I get it," Jonah said.

"No, you've no idea."

"I know what Bennett did," Jonah said, his voice fierce. He glanced over at Beau. "We all do."

I tried to shake my head, but it hurt too much. "It wasn't my choice," I said again. "I don't care how many times they told me in rehab that it was my responsibility, it wasn't."

"You trusted him," Beau said, nodding. My younger brother always had a knack for getting right to the point you still struggled to make. It was like he knew your thoughts before you were done thinking them. We always called him creepy for it, but I was grateful for it now as I struggled through the haze of pain. "He was our manager, we were kids, we were raised to trust adults. No one had ever betrayed us like that before."

"Fuck," I breathed. It still felt humiliating to think back on how it all had happened. The first time Bennett—our manager and the man who'd shepherded our career from county fairs to giant stadiums—offered me a pill to "take the edge off" I hadn't thought twice. Fame was a fickle bitch and Bennett said he was only looking out for me when he handed me the white pills and the glass of water.

Whether it was his aim to get me addicted and therefore beholden to him or whether that was just a happy side effect to his carelessness, I'll never know. "I still think about it. Every fucking day I catch myself wanting to use again."

I heard Finn growl softly. Beau and Jonah looked at each other, but my sister just looked down. I wondered what Claire was thinking. She'd always been desperately jealous of our fame. Fame she'd been shut out of for being a girl. Bennett had wanted a boy band. No room for a girl, no matter how talented a singer she was.

If she was listening right now, really fucking listening, maybe she'd start realizing the fame wasn't worth the cost?

"When I got sober, they were always talking about how I chose to take this path, but I never did," I went on. My legs were throbbing in time with my heartbeat. "Now, here I am being asked to take pills again because they say I have no choice! That I'm not going to be able to do it on my own." I looked at each of my siblings so they would know I was dead serious. "I am. I'll take the risk."

Beau and Jonah glanced at each other. "Sometimes I feel like Bennett fucked you over worse than Noelle did," Jonah said.

At the mention of my ex, both visibly winced. "She gave an interview," Claire said through clenched teeth. "Fucking bitch didn't even mention you at all."

"Why would she?" I sighed. "She got what she needed from me. A springboard to fame."

"Well her new song sucks and she does the fucking robot in her music video. All 'teehee look at me I'm adorably awkward.'" Claire rolled her eyes viciously. She folded her arms over her chest. "I wish like hell I could run into her sometime," she said loyally. "She's gonna catch these hands." She waved her slim, piano-playing hands with their perfectly pink manicure around like a karate master.

Even though I felt like shit and even though it hurt like hell it still made me smile to see my baby sister playing badass. Made me smile enough that it took me a second to register what she'd just said. Noelle had a new single out.

I have to watch that.

I can't watch that.

I licked my lips and tried to grin wider. "For her own safety I hope she never crosses paths with you."

"Oh my posse is on the case, G-man," she said with a decisive nod. "Willa, Sadie, Ruby, and I are ready to lay down the little-sister-law."

"Wait, Ruby's in this posse?" Jonah interjected, looking worried.

Claire rolled her eyes. "I won't let your future wife get dinged up. But you have to know she's a good scrapper."

"I am well aware," he said, rubbing the back of his neck and looking way too delighted by the idea. Just looking at him you could tell he was picturing his fiancée in some kind of ninja catsuit kicking ass.

I groaned.

"You okay?" Beau asked.

"No," I complained. "Jonah's making me nauseous."

Finn burst out laughing as Jonah smiled sheepishly and I felt something like gratitude in my chest that all five of us were talking again, that we were in the same room. Even if the room was my mom's cramped little sunroom where my bed took up most of the space.

"But hey," Beau broke in, interrupting Finn giving Jonah epic shit about Ruby's bad taste in men, "You said you're overdue for your ibuprofen, right?"

"I'll go get it," Claire volunteered, glaring at Jonah. "Whatever your train of thought is about my best friend right now, please, for my sake, make it derail." She stalked from the room while Finn hooted.

But as much as I loved it when Jonah was brought down a peg, I wasn't feeling up to joining in. "Fucking hate this," I said to no one in particular. "Wish I could get up and get my own damn ibuprofen." Then I brightened when I remembered something. "But then again," I said, looking up at my brothers. "I walked today, did I tell you?"

Beau clapped his hand together. "Shit, really?"

"That's incredible!" Jonah added, pumping his fist. Finn raised his above his head in a fuck-yeah salute.

I grinned. "Ten steps and then I basically fell on Everly," I said, neglecting to mention how good she had felt in my arms. The curve of her spine at her lower back urging me to slide my hand further down. The way her eyes had shone when I told her I remembered her, with a kind of open, hopeful expression that was both pants-tightening and heart-breaking at the same time. I blinked. "But still, I fucking walked and I'll be able to do more soon.

"No wonder you're hurting." Claire had returned with my pills. I hadn't realized she'd been listening but then again, this was Claire we were talking about. She always had her nose in other people's business. "That's a lot for your first therapy appointment."

"I'm fine," I said as I swallowed them dry. It must have been the millionth time I said those two words, but no one believed me.

"You could try something that wasn't an opioid," Beau piped up. He'd been scrolling through my tablet. "Non-addictive stuff. Tor-a-dol," he sounded out. "Or semi-opioids like Tra-ma-dol or Tap-en-ta-dol." He grimaced. "I have no idea if I'm saying them right but you could at least *try* to make this process easier on you."

"Non-opioid, like the ibuprofen I just took?" I stuck out my tongue. "I took my meds, doc. I'm a good little pill-head."

"It's not the same," Beau said. He looked genuinely pained to see me in pain. I'd been completely out of it during the first stages of my recovery, but I somehow knew he'd been at my side the most.

I gritted my teeth and shook my head. "Sorry man," I said. I wanted so badly to agree with Beau. He'd always been the caretaker. Of all of my siblings he was the most in tune with how we were feeling. I trusted him, I always trusted him. But not about this. "I can't do it. I really, really can't."

"Stay strong," Finn said. He glanced at his twin as if he too saw this as a betrayal of Beau's status as the one who knew about these things. "I know what he went through, man, and I don't want you to fuck up your recovery in any way." Finn leaned back against the wall. "Still wanna kick his ass, you know," he said, letting his head fall back.

"Who? Bennett?"

"You never let me take him out the way I wanted to," my hotheaded little brother grunted.

Claire was nodding her head. "I agree with Finn," she said, because of course she did. The two of them should have been the twins. They were more alike than any of the rest of us. "How about we just go break Bennett's ankles too? Would that make you feel better? Tit for tat. He gets you hooked on pills, we get him hooked up to an IV." It was hard to remember her in pink dresses with bows in her hair when her eyes had that bloodthirsty gleam in them. She glanced at Jonah. "I'm sure Ruby would be up for joining us."

I looked at my siblings, ready even now to go kick some ass for me. I tried to smile, but it hurt too much. "No," I said, the words of recovery still ringing through my head. "Thanks guys, but..." I sighed. "This is on me."

Chapter Eight

EVERLY

I needed to leave right now if I was going to make it across town in time for class. I grabbed my heavy bag and headed towards the back door off the kitchen, intending to sneak around the side of the house so the sound of the front door opening wouldn't wake my parents.

But the second I stepped into the kitchen, I heard the telltale thump of my mother's feet on the floor upstairs.

Which meant I had woken her up.

Fuck. She was going to want to talk to me. Which meant I was going to be late.

"Hey," I exhaled as she blinked and yawned her way down the stairs, performing the part of "aggrieved parent woken too soon" perfectly. My mother missed her calling when she opened a bakery rather than moving to Hollywood to star in old-fashioned, overly emotive silent films.

"I heard you were home," she sighed pointedly. "I didn't want to miss seeing you. You're like a ghost in this house."

I sank back onto my heels. The issue here was that my class schedule, and now my new job next door, had me out of the house most of the day. In a normal family this would mean we could relax together in the evening, unwinding as we shared stories of our day. But that would never happen for two reasons. Number one was that my parents were in bed by seven. And number two was that there was no guilt-free relaxing in the Foster home.

But both of these reasons were facts of my life that were never going to change, so I just shrugged. "Yeah, sorry," I said, and bent to retie my shoes.

She yawned and stretched again as she headed to the coffee maker. "You headed back out?" she asked, as casually as can be.

I paused, steadying my hands, then resumed tying the laces. "Yeah," I said, breezy and easy, giving her the benefit of the doubt. "Class is at 3:45."

"You have class today?" my mom interrupted.

Her back was still to me. She reached up into the cupboard to retrieve her mug, then tapped her foot, waiting for the coffee maker to heat up. She couldn't see me staring at her in disbelief. "Yeah, Mom. I've had class on Thursday afternoons all semester."

When she finally did turn around, her expression was halfway between bored and irritated. "You didn't tell me," she said, shaking her head. She blew on her coffee and then took a sip.

For a moment the only sound was the whip of the March winds lashing sheets of rain against the window panes. It made me feel even more claustrophobic than I usually did in this house. "I definitely did," I said, deliberately keeping my tone mild as I finished tying my shoes, and stood up. "It's been this way since January." I brushed my hands down the front of my scrubs, wordlessly pointing them out to her, if she'd only look at me.

There was always that hope when I wore my scrubs around my mom like this. That she'd smile and say something about how she was proud of me. But my mom considered my nursing school uniform nothing more than some kind of delayed teenaged rebellion. Like at twenty-two I was still going through a stage and would wise up eventually.

So when she shook her head, I shouldn't have been disappointed, but I was anyway. Disappointment was as natural to me as my broad, strong shoulders and the star-shaped birthmark under my right clavicle. It was part of me. "I would have remembered," my mother said, and I could see by the obstinate jut of her chin that she was starting to get angry at me for pointing out that she'd screwed up. "You need to be better at communicating."

I licked my lips, wondering just how invested I needed to be in this fight. "Sorry, Mom," I said instead.

She nodded, victorious without even having to drag out the big guns. Then she glanced over to the counter and sighed at the pile of mail my dad had left before heading up for his nap. "Be home by curfew," she said distractedly.

"Yup," I said, unnatural irritation making my fingers itch. "Hey mom, I forgot to tell you," I said as she tore open an envelope with her fingernail. "I met up with a couple of the God's Chosen cult ladies yesterday. I'm joining up."

"Sounds good," she murmured, intently scouring a piece of junk mail.

I licked my lips. "Cool. Bye then."

Those extra three minutes spent talking to her ended up snowballing. You give the Grim Reaper one inch and he takes a yard. The second my car thought it was acceptable to stall, it started doing it with gusto, with every stoplight between my house and the campus an exercise in extreme praying. When I finally found a spot half a mile from my building, I checked the clock on my phone.

Class was starting right now.

I broke out into a full-on sprint. The rain pelted me with icy needles, sizzling as it hit my overheated skin while I skidded through puddles.

Once inside the building, the hallways felt overwarm, and the rainwater on my skin mixed with the prickles of sweat. I was now six minutes late, and that was enough to make it so my entrance had everyone swiveling in their seats.

Our regular professor was out today. The substitute paused and gave me a pointed look as I sat down. I'd missed her introduction.

That turned out to be the only time she looked at me the entire period.

"Like I said," she rehashed unnecessarily as I found my way to the back of the lecture hall. "Professor Dorrington just asked me to go over some common questions you're going to see on the boards."

I straightened up in my seat. I'd been studying at least two hours a day for months now. This would be easy for me. I'd been studying. I knew the answers.

But I seemed invisible.

"First question!" she read off her index card. "When caring for a patient with a cardiac dysrhythmia, which laboratory value is a priority for the healthcare provider to monitor?"

"Sodium, potassium, and calcium," I muttered just as the blonde down in the front flubbed it.

I pressed my lips together. The instructor asked for another answer. I raised my hand first, but she swept past me and called on Jamie-with-the-shiny-hair who didn't even have her hand raised. Jamie haltingly gave the answer while I mouthed along with her.

The next question was even easier. I remembered it word for word from my NCLEX practice quizzes online. "The healthcare provider is seeing four patients at the neighborhood clinic. Which of these patients should the healthcare provider identify to be most at risk for iron-deficiency anemia?" she called out. "Number one: The woman of childbearing age reporting a craving for ice. Number two: The obese patient with a history of gastric bypass surgery. Number three: The patient who follows a strict vegan diet. Or number four: The patient who has a diagnosis of chronic renal failure?"

I knew this one, and confidently threw up my hand.

"The vegan," one of the few male nurses shouted. "Need to check them for b12 too, since they don't eat meat." He shook his head. "Stupid vegans."

The sub grinned but shook her head. "Wrong. Anyone else?"

I was practically straining my shoulder trying to get her to call on me. The answer was the woman of childbearing age. I knew my periods were heavy enough to bring on anemia. I knew this question on a personal level.

"Okay you guys, the answer is the woman of childbearing age!" the sub shouted. "Heavy menstrual flow can bring on anemia. Definitely need to go back and review that. All of you." She flipped through her cards, wrinkling her nose as she did.

I felt a flush crawl across my face.

I wasn't certain why today, of all days, it bothered me that I was being overlooked. I certainly should have expected it. Slipping by in the background, stepping aside for others to go into the spotlight, that was my specialty. It had never bothered me before. It didn't even bother me that Gabe hadn't remembered who I was when he had his arms around me. It didn't. It definitely didn't.

"I noticed you," he'd said.

I shook my head and tried to drag my struggling brain back to the classroom. It had devolved into pandemonium now, with one older student outright crying that she was never going to pass, there was no way she was going to pass.

I turned to smile at her, reassuringly, but someone else stepped in and gave her a hug.

I turned back to my seat and fiddled with my pen.

The clock ticked as I sat in silence for the rest of the class. Not even trying to answer. If I thought that maybe not raising my hand would make her call on me, I was wrong. I may as well have just not shown up at all. When class was finally over, I slowly gathered my things as people gossiped and called to each other around me. I hadn't gotten to know any of my classmates. It hadn't seemed necessary, but today that same feeling of wanting to be noticed had me seeing them as if for the first time, as if I'd just woken up with the semester nearly over and realized I'd moved through it like a ghost. I looked around, hoping to make eye contact with someone, hoping to make that connection I'd been missing.

I may not have met very many people in class, but I'd observed enough of it to understand the hierarchy. The guys and the continuing ed people, the older women who looked frazzled and left class with phones jammed in their ears as they raced to pick up Johnny from daycare, all sat behind me. In the front row were the A-students, the girls who challenged the professor every chance they got, doing their best Hermione from Harry Potter impressions.

It was the ones who sat in the middle, not so close as to be nerdy but not so far back as to be overlooked, that had the most social capital. In my head I called them the blondes. They all had different hair colors, of course, but they were all blonde in spirit.

I sat in a row by myself. Not belonging to any of the groups.

I took a deep breath and looked down at the blondes as they packed their pretty purses, and I smiled at the one with the shiniest hair.

Her eyes slid right over me. Not even bothering to give me her contempt. Just flat out ignoring me.

I licked my lips, unsurprised.

I'd never known the code, the secret series of knocks that let you enter the world of friends and attention. There was something about me, a smell, a fault, that set me apart, marked me as an outsider. I was too blunt, too honest. I didn't understand how to smooth things, how not to say exactly what it was that crossed my mind. Afraid of being awkward, I tended to stay silent, which in turn only made me more awkward when I opened my mouth.

I sat back down again, grabbing for my phone like I'd just received a text. I smiled down at my blank screen, miming reading a message as all my classmates took off in clumps of twos and threes, calling to each other as they passed me while I mimed typing a reply. Maybe they knew I was faking but it felt better than letting them know I was alone. Better to stay silent than embarrass myself by opening my mouth. I rifled through my bag, arranging notes, my cheeks burning. I wouldn't watch them. I was tired of always watching.

I wanted someone to fucking notice me for once.

The classroom was quiet now, the heavy tick of the radiator the only sound. Outside, the everpresent rain pattered softly, like a whisper, against the window. I swallowed hard. I could see all my classmates with their brightly colored, ruffled umbrellas heading out for their cars.

That was another thing wrong with me. I never remembered a fucking umbrella.

The door swung back open again. I glanced up, moving my thumbs over the keyboard in case one of them was returning. But I saw the bright yellow of the janitor's cart.

The regular cleaner didn't usually come until night, which was why I glanced up again, wondering if it was Nilda and planning on asking about her dogs. She barely spoke English, but it felt nice to have her smile at me.

But behind it was a girl about my age. She was pretty in a plain, forthright way, her hair back in French braid like a girl much younger than her would wear.

I smiled at her.

She stopped, looking panicked that I was still sitting there and backed out again rather than talk to me.

It appeared I was marked as an outsider even by the custodial staff.

Flushing, I gathered my books and headed out the back entrance and into the rain.

Chapter Nine

EVERLY

A week later, I slammed the door to the kitchen shut and flew to the table while unzipping my schoolbag at the same time. I didn't have much time.

Between running Gabe to PT, clinical, and last-minute cramming for my boards on Thursday, I had nearly forgotten about the unit test. I cracked open my beat-up laptop and signed into the system to download my open-book test. It was due into my instructor's inbox by midnight. It was five in the evening and I still had Gabe's nighttime dressing change to take care of and reading for tomorrow's class.

I took a deep breath. I had time. I was going to get this done.

I started clicking through the test, feeling dread pool in my belly with each successive question. "Wait," I breathed, leaning in and squinting at the screen while my cursor blinked away in silent judgment. "Is that a trick question?" I flicked through my notes, tracing my finger down the page and tapping what I thought was the answer, but the wording was off. I read the question aloud to myself again, noisily exhaling out the tension as I did. "Shit," I murmured and clicked the answer I was sixty-five percent sure was correct, but the fact that I wasn't one-hundred percent sure made me even more anxious than before. "Shit," I repeated, that single word becoming almost like a mantra. "Shit, shit, shit." I clicked to the next question and prayed.

The door in from the garage banged open.

I startled, knocking my water bottle to the floor where it clattered with a loud, tinny bang, but blessedly did not spill. I clenched my teeth together and then looked up at my parents. "You guys are back already?" I said, trying to sound happy about it and failing miserably.

My mother's nostrils flared a little at the obvious distress in my voice, but she put her smile back on, choosing to dismiss it. "There was a wait," she said. "We would've been there past seven."

I exhaled and shook my head, trying to look sympathetic through my irritation. My parents never stayed out past seven. It had been a hard and fast rule, ever since I was a child, that life stopped at 7 o'clock. Growing up this had been fine because I was on their same schedule, but now that I had night classes, and practicum and clinical, it was something else entirely. Plus I was in the middle of a freaking unit test. "Huh," I said, my heart sinking. Because I knew what came next.

Slam went my mother's pocketbook on the counter. *Whack* went the closet door as it hit the wall. The TV blared to immediate life, loud enough for each explosion from the movie they'd started last night to rattle my teeth. "Start the stove," my father bellowed at my mom, as he yanked open the freezer. "There's a pizza in here at least."

"Honestly, I cannot believe how rude that hostess was," my mom complained as she slammed through her drawer full of pots and pans. "If I talked to my customers that way I'd be out of business. Everly? Scooch your stuff over?" When I took too long, she came over and gave all my notebooks a nudge.

I took a deep breath, and kept my eyes firmly on my screen so they wouldn't see the frustrated tears that glittered in them. "Hey, guys? I just need twenty more minutes to finish this test, okay? You know the WiFi is terrible in my room, and I have to get this done. Could you keep it down until then?"

No answer. I didn't have to turn my head to know that my mom was probably staring me down. I wanted to swallow but my throat felt way too tight.

The explosions boomed from the living room.

I waited a beat. Waited for my parents to give me hell.

Then I looked up and realized they weren't even in the room anymore.

They hadn't heard me.

I sat back in the chair, uncertain of how I felt about that. I should have been relieved that they didn't hear me, but I was more pissed than anything else.

On the screen, my cursor blinked in time with the seconds that were ticking away. Another explosion made the glasses in the cabinet rattle.

I leaped to my feet. Without even understanding what I was doing, I started packing my bag up. "I'm heading out!" I called.

No one answered. No one noticed I was leaving. And for once I was happy about that.

Chapter Ten

GABE

Once I was able to manage stairs on my crutches, I had insisted on being moved to my old bedroom. Being in the sunroom made me feel like a guest in my house, and I was keenly aware of my family trying to tiptoe around whenever I slept. I didn't want them to have to worry about waking me anymore.

I also really, really missed having a door I could shut.

So my brothers had banded together with my dad to wrestle the awful hospital bed up the stairs. They'd managed to keep the cursing to a minimum, though when they set it down on Finn's foot, he'd let off a few choice f-bombs that my mother pretended not to hear.

I was finally alone again, and though it felt weird to be away from the bustle of the house, it was so much easier to fall asleep in the silence.

I have no idea how long I was out when I was woken by an unfamiliar noise. Like a mouse had gotten trapped in the wall.

Scratch scratch scratch.

We had mice growing up. It's one of the inevitabilities of living in the country. They came in, like clockwork, every November, something you could set your watch by. The mice would come, and my father would diligently set out his traps, and my mother would squeal and run away shuddering every time one of the little guillotines snapped shut. As my brothers and I got older, checking the traps became our job, something Finn always took a rather unhealthy interest in.

I was used to mice, but they were annoying when I was trying to take a nap. Without even opening my eyes, I reached out and balled my good fist. Then I slammed it hard against my bedroom wall, intending to scare it away. *Scratch scratch scratch, BANG!*

"Jesus!" came a voice.

I opened my eyes in surprise. Someone was in my room? "The fuck?" I managed to croak. I opened my eyes and Everly Foster was on the floor of my room, a drift of papers and books all across her lap. She looked up at me guiltily. "Hi."

I wondered if she knew I'd been dreaming about her. "Hey," I said, trying to sit up.

"Sorry. I thought you were asleep," she said.

"I was asleep," I said, rubbing my eyes. "But the mouse woke me up."

She wrinkled her nose. "Mouse?"

"Yeah."

She shook her head. "I didn't hear a mouse," she said, turning back to her paper and writing something down.

That's when I realized the scratching sound was that of her pencil and the skittery sound that I'd thought was dripping water from the gutters outside was actually her fingers dancing over her keyboard.

"What are you doing here?" I asked, trying to sound curious. I didn't mind her being here. Not one bit.

"Trying," she said, pausing to read something on her screen and then click, "to finish a unit test." She exhaled and let her head fall back against the wall and gave me a look of such utter helplessness I wanted to leap from the bed and go fight all her battles for her.

This girl was starting to get under my skin.

"Sorry," she sighed. "It's noisy at my house and it was quiet here, and I needed to change your dressing anyway before I headed into clinical but you were asleep and I just saw a golden opportunity to finally work uninterrupted." She leaned in and clicked the screen again, this time with a satisfied grin on her face. "Okay phew, that one was easy."

"Who's being noisy at your house?" I wondered.

"My parents," she said without taking her eyes from her screen.

I grimaced as I rolled over and sat stiffly at the edge of the bed. She didn't look right down there on my floor. A girl with her dignity, with her sass? There was something about this scenario that set my teeth on edge. "Wait, your parents are the ones being noisy when you have to study?" I asked, lowering my voice halfway through the question when I realized I wasn't exactly helping her concentration by badgering her about this. But honestly, what the fuck?

She nodded, clicking three times in rapid succession. Then she widened her eyes and let out a long exhale that made the baby curls around her face dance. No matter how quiet her face was, there was still always something about her that was in motion. "I'm done," she said with a relieved smile.

I grinned back at her, feeling strangely relieved myself. "Good. But I'm sorry you had to sit on the floor of my bedroom to finish it."

She shrugged and sat up. "I'll clean up," she said, starting to pack all her papers.

"No, that's not what I was talking about," I said, waving my hand at her to stop. "I was wondering why your parents didn't keep it down when you had to study. Did you tell them to—?"

"Tell them to keep it down?" she supplied. "Doesn't really work that way," she said dryly.

I narrowed my eyes. "They do know you're going to school, right? Working your ass off? That whole thing?"

Her smile was equal parts amused and frustrated. "I mean, I think they have a vague notion," she said.

Frustrated, I stared at her, all huddled on my floor doing her absolute best. It wasn't right. "You need to get your own place," I said, snapping the fingers of my good hand.

"Yeah, no shit," she said.

"You've thought about it? It would make things a lot easier for you."

"Yeah, thanks for the advice," she said, with a dismissive wave of her hand. "It's not like I'm rolling in money."

"There're plenty of cheap places," I said, which was a total lie. I had no idea if there were cheap places or not. Feeling like a tool, I shut my mouth.

Everly just shook her head. "Only way I could do it is if I found a roommate, I think. I need to save all my money for classes. Plus my car is about to die any second."

I could hear the frustration in her voice and it pissed me off. This chick had everything going for her, but it was like she was swimming upstream. Unsupportive parents, shitty transportation, no place to even get peace and quiet so she could study. I hated the worry lines that creased her face, and I also hated that I knew how tired she was, and could only blame myself for part of it. "You can study right here from now on," I told her. "It's not like I'm going to be getting up and bothering you."

I expected her to smile, but she just turned and gave me a serious look. "I'll make it up. You don't have to pay me for tonight."

"Shut the fuck up," I growled. "You need a break, and I think it's high time someone gave you a break, don't you think?" I grinned at her. "Now come sit on the bed here. I want to make sure that you spend your time here well. Pop quiz."

Chapter Eleven

EVERLY

I perched at the side of his bed and settled my textbook on my lap. Gabe was watching me carefully, all his attention trained on me like a spotlight on the star of the show.

I looked down and noticed my hand was crumpling the page. I hurriedly swiped at it to flatten the crumpled corners, and Gabe's eyes followed the motion.

He was making me jittery and nervous and I had no idea why.

Yes I did.

Was he remembering that night? In these past few weeks, I'd pushed it so far back in my brain that it seemed to circle back around to the forefront. The way he was looking at me right now, I almost believed he was remembering.

He flicked his tongue out, wetting his lips. I held my breath, waiting for the revelation that he'd known all along.

"You know everything in that book?" he asked, a little glint of mischief in his eyes.

I blinked at the unexpected question but quickly recovered. "Of course," I said, a touch more indignantly than I wanted. "My boards are in two days. I know it backwards and forwards."

His hand shot out a lot faster than I was expecting and the next thing I knew he was reading aloud. "A patient diagnosed with ulcerative colitis is admitted to the medical unit. When assessing the patient, which of these findings would be of the most concern?" He cleared his throat. "Rebound tenderness, Oral temperature of ninety-nine degrees Fahrenheit," he raised an eyebrow, "which is thirty-seven degrees Celsius but of course you knew that."

"Of course." I nodded.

"Let's see...oh, jeez, I don't even know how to say that so I hope it's not the answer or..." he wrinkled his nose theatrically. "Or bloody diarrhea?"

I grinned in triumph. "Rebound tenderness," I said promptly.

He closed the book with an emphatic thud. "I disagree."

"You disagree with the NCLEX?"

"Bloody diarrhea is always a concern," he said, looking thoroughly grossed out.

"I had no idea you'd be such a priss, Gabe King. I guess that's why I'm the nurse and you're not." I reached over and tugged my precious study materials from his hand.

He relinquished them easily. "I'm thinking this gig you have right now is a lot easier than what you'd normally have to deal with, huh?"

I arched an eyebrow at him. "The gig itself is a cakewalk. It's the patient that's difficult."

"Aw, whaddya mean? I'm super easy." His eyes fell to my lips in a way that didn't seem at all accidental. "Haven't even asked you for a sponge bath yet."

My heart stilled a moment. I raised the other eyebrow at him.

His smile was completely innocent. Too innocent when he said, "To be honest, since I fell, I haven't exactly felt safe in the bathroom."

I stared at him. That was certainly a valid concern, especially with the weakness in his ankles. But why did it seem like his eyes were gleaming? "Do you have a fever?" I blurted.

"I'm definitely feeling warm," he said. Again with the innocent smile.

I pressed my hand to his forehead. He closed his eyes. "You look flushed," I said, noting the heat rising from his skin. I swallowed. "Have you taken your ibuprofen?"

He opened his eyes. "You look a little flushed too, Everly."

"I'm fine." I was decidedly not fine. Because helping him bathe was definitely on my list of tasks I was expected to do. Unbidden my mind forced me to relive the moments of seeing him sprawled naked on the ground. His...his... I blushed furiously and turned away. "I'll run you a bath."

I practically fled from his room. Once in the bathroom, I ran the tap for a second, then splashed the cold water on my face. I was cracking up. The pressure of the boards. I had only kissed Gabe that night because he was Jonah's brother. It was the closest I could get to the man I'd been yearning for half my life. And when he hadn't remembered, hadn't said anything, I thought I was safe. Just a bad decision chalked up to one too many rum and Cokes. Wasn't that something all normal girls had in their past? A rum-and-Coke fueled mistake? I'd kissed the wrong guy at a bar and then disappeared. Surely that wasn't a crime? No one was hurt. It should just be something I put behind me.

So why was I thinking about doing it again?

It wasn't because I'd seen him naked. No. I wasn't that type of girl. I didn't go to pieces at the thought of a hot guy.

I stared at myself in the mirror, wide-eyed. Since when had I ever thought of Gabe as hot?

I turned and purposefully cranked the faucet in the bathtub. Then I closed my eyes and tried not to remember the way he had looked. I wasn't remembering those muscles and scars and tattoos and, oh, god, did he want me to wash him? Why did this feel like something I shouldn't be asked to do? Why did this feel like something I really wanted to do?

When the tub was near to full, I turned it off and tested the temperature with my elbow. I would assist him in getting into the tub. And then...and then I'd supervise. He'd regained enough mobility in his arm to wash himself. There was no need for me to run a cloth over his naked torso or let the cloth dip lower and...

Now I was fleeing the bathroom too. At least I was getting my cardio in today.

When I returned to his bedroom, I saw that he was sitting up on his own.

Clad only in his boxers.

The long scar on the left side of his ribcage still made me wince to see it, but it was completely closed now, a deep purple river winding its way around his chest. For a single moment, I could envision how it would feel under my lips, the knotted skin warm and alive as I traced it with my tongue. It was so clear and detailed that I startled back from him before I realized I hadn't moved at all.

"You all right there, Nurse?"

"You need to be wearing your boots," I barked.

He grinned as if my hardass-nurse routine didn't fool him at all. "Kristyn said I can have them off as much as I can stand these days." This time his eyes lingered on my lips for much longer than a heartbeat. "And if you're there to make sure I don't fall then I think I'm okay."

Slowly he stood up. When he winced, I caught my breath, but then he smiled again. "I'm okay." He stretched out his arm to me. "Gonna need you right here though."

If it was obvious how quickly I moved to his side, he at least had the good grace not to say anything about it. His arm settled as a heavy, pleasant weight over my shoulders. Without thinking, I inhaled deeply. "I wouldn't do that," he chuckled.

"You smell good," I said automatically, then paused when I realized what I'd said. With his arm across my shoulder, I was supposed to be supporting him, but I felt very much like he was in control. Like he was the one who was holding on to me.

"Okay," he said. "Here we go."

He stepped slowly and carefully, not rushing or overdoing it for once. But we still reached the bathroom far too soon. When his arm was off me I sighed a little.

"Hope the water's nice and hot," he said.

"I mean, it was. It's probably cooled down by now." There was something about being so close to him in this tiny space that was making my breath come faster.

"Can you heat things up for me?"

I blinked when I realized I was staring at how green his eyes looked instead of answering his question. "What?" Then I realized what his question actually was. "What?" I repeated, a little more loudly now.

He ran his tongue along his top teeth, making his smile look almost predatory. "I mean, I can't bend over and turn on the hot water. I'm afraid I'll lose my balance." He paused. "So can you heat it up for me?"

"Oh." I hoped the steam was a good enough excuse for why I was flushed.

"What did you think I meant?" he prodded.

"Nothing." I bent over, let some of the now-cooled water out, and ran the hot water again. As I was bent over, I was acutely aware of the position I was in, how the two of us were aligned. I scooted all the way against the wall and straightened back up again. I stepped behind him without looking him in the eye. Doing so felt very dangerous.

"Thanks," he said.

And then he pulled down his boxers.

Goddamn this man and his complete nonchalance about nudity. I looked away from him and then, remembering that this was my job and nothing more, I forced myself to stare straight ahead. But even with my eyes trained at a point on the wall, I still caught a glimpse of his smooth, muscled back and the strong, round heft of his ass. I'd never been one to ogle men's butts but I was suddenly a devout ass-woman.

"Kettlebell," Gabe said out of nowhere.

"Huh?" I continued staring straight ahead.

"You're wondering how to get an ass like mine, I can tell. I'll tell you the secret. A big mean guy named Carlos yelled at me until I could do squats with a kettlebell."

"I wasn't wondering anything of the sort."

"Why else were you staring at my ass, Nurse?"

"Checking your balance," I said, sounding almost convincing. "His name is Carlos, huh? And he was mean to you?"

"Not as mean as you, but close."

I couldn't help it, I laughed aloud. The biggest, freest laugh I had laughed all day long. Gabe grinned at me as I shook my head.

"You think I'm mean, huh?"

“Nah. I think you’re pretty sweet, actually.”

I swallowed. A sharp retort sprang to my lips and then died there unsaid. No one had ever called me sweet before. No one had ever called me cute, or adorable, but Gabe sure acted like I was both. And I looked forward to it. I looked forward to the way he looked at me without getting distracted by anything else. It felt heady, almost addicting. I wanted his attention on me. Even though the rain had been pouring down for weeks, when I was with Gabe I felt like the sun was shining full on my face.

“Here,” I said, kneeling down and unstrapping his boot. “You need to get these off.” As I knelt I could feel the heat off his leg. I was very close to him. Very very close to his nakedness. I tugged at the Velcro. “Just step out of them now, I’ve got you,” I said as I straightened up. “Lean on me now, I’ve got you.”

“I know you do,” he murmured, barely audible. I wasn’t sure I was even supposed to hear it, but I had, and it made something strange and new swell in my chest.

Chapter Twelve

EVERLY

I dragged my hand across my notepaper and suddenly it was Gabe's skin again.

For the fifteenth time since class started, warmth was spreading through my body, an insistent heat that pooled in my belly and made my nipples tighten. I sat up in my seat, crossed and recrossed my legs and tried like hell to pay attention to the last review before the boards tomorrow.

But the second my hand moved again, it was as if it was holding a washcloth and running against smooth, tanned skin, the texture of sparse golden hairs running like silk against my fingertips. The instructor's voice faded to mere static in the background.

I licked my lips and stretched my fingers out. There had been nothing erotic about the bath. Nothing except his naked body, nothing except the way his eyes closed when he sank into the water. There had been nothing sensuous except the soft moan that fell from his lips when I let the cloth brush across his shoulder. He was my patient and I was providing a level of care that justified my high weekly rate. That was all. There was nothing forbidden about the way his eyes fluttered open and he looked at me with that grin playing about his lips and said, "Thanks Nurse."

There was nothing strange about how he was wearing no clothes at all but I was the one who felt naked.

A sudden burst of noise around me jolted me out of my reverie. I looked around and to my horror everyone was packing up already.

Class was over and I had spent my entire review thinking about Gabe King's naked body.

I'd missed my final review.

I stood up and started packing up my unused laptop, trying not to pay attention to the low thrum of panic that was now humming through my ears. But my fingers betrayed me, becoming useless and shaking with the tips nothing but pins and needles.

I held my breath. This wasn't the first time this had happened, although it had been a while. My sister Abby had called this fun little party trick of mind "floppy hands." It came on when I was stressed or not getting enough sleep.

I sat down and rested my traitorous hands on my knees while I waited for them to stop shaking. It would pass. It always passed. I breathed out and tried not to think about what the doc on my clinical had said when I'd nonchalantly asked him about it, pretending it was a question for the boards. "Oh, you mean like an essential tremor? Yeah, you'd definitely want to get that looked at."

My hands had randomly shaken my whole life, but I only just learned it was a problem this semester.

As I sat in my desk chair, I watched Professor Dorrington scrolling across her laptop screen with a pursed-lip look of concentration on her face. "Nurse Foster?" she called out to me.

Startled, I tried to press my hands into my thighs, but they still flopped around in my lap like fish out of water. "Yes?" I said, wondering what on earth had led her to notice me on today of all days.

She glanced up, seemingly miffed that I was still in my seat. "I was just checking through my grading. Were you planning on handing in your unit test sometime soon?"

It was like someone had poured a bucket of icewater over my head. I froze to the spot, and then started shaking right along with my hands. An anxiety attack. I was seconds away from a full-blown anxiety attack.

I was a nurse. I knew what to do. But knowing what to do and being able to do it were two separate things. As Professor Dorrington looked over the top of her half-moon glasses to peer critically at me, I desperately tried to get air into my lungs, but it felt like someone was squeezing my chest too tight. "I..." I gulped. "Did?"

"I beg to differ," she called from way down below me. This was ridiculous, the two of us shouting across the empty lecture hall, but I couldn't move. I wasn't sure I could put one foot in front of another without collapsing. And her pride wouldn't allow her to come to me. She raised her voice a little louder. "Every day that it's late it gets marked down twenty percent."

Panic squirted a bright hot metallic taste in my mouth. It'd been a day already and I needed to keep my grade up as high as I could. "I sent it in," I said as clearly as I could around the thickness of my tongue. In the bright hot glare of the impending panic attack, the harder she looked at me, the more I felt like I was lying. Shaking my head, I tore my eyes away from hers, and pulled out my phone, holding it tight in violently shaking hands. "I'm looking right here, in my sent folder," I said. "The timestamp is 7:48 PM."

A heavy silence fell over us as she turned back to her computer. I felt like I couldn't move, pinned down by the weight of her implied accusation. My hands shook so hard that even sitting on them wasn't enough. My whole body was slicked down in perspiration and I was gasping like a marathon runner as Professor Dorrington silently and judgmentally scrolled through her inbox. It was right then, in the middle of my silent breakdown, that the door to the lecture hall banged open and the same French-braided girl from before stood there with the heavy yellow cart.

And for some reason, I was able to catch my breath.

Maybe it was the expression on her face, the serene composure, the shy glance. Maybe it was the blessed distraction from my silent standoff with my professor. Or maybe it was the small play of a smile across her lips when she looked at me. Like the look of recognition you give to someone right before you open your mouth and reveal you don't actually know their name.

She turned her heavy cart into the hall and then stopped short when she noticed that Professor Dorrington was still at her desk. "Oh!" she said and jerked her cart back in surprise. The force of it sent the mops that were on the front clattering to the floor.

Without thinking, I jumped to my feet. And to my surprise, my hand closed firmly on the fallen mop and didn't show any signs of tremor at all. "Here," I said, handing her the one, and then the other. "I got you," I said. They were heavier than they looked.

At that moment, Professor Dorrington slapped her laptop closed and stood up. The custodian girl and I both startled and looked at her.

The expression on her face was one of studied boredom. "You're all set, Nurse Foster," she sniffed as she shrugged on her complicated wool coat.

I inhaled a deep, full breath. "You saw it then? My test?" For some reason I glanced at the custodian girl. She was watching us both with keen interest.

"Like I said, you're all set." Professor Dorrington grabbed her case and turned to stalk out the main entrance.

I let out that full breath and looked at the custodian again, and for some reason the urge to laugh overtook me. "Oh my god that was the scariest moment in my entire life," I gasped, falling back to sit down on one of the empty chairs.

"She's terrifying," the custodian whispered with her eyes wide. "Thanks for your help."

I glanced at her and she quickly looked down, avoiding my eyes. Her braid was so tight it pulled the sides of her face taut. I found myself wanting to know why she wore it that way. The only people I knew who braided their hair like that were little girls for dance recitals and the creepy cult ladies who moved in packs through town, not talking to anyone except themselves. "I'm Everly," I said, holding out my hand. "You might have already heard my professor yelling my last name, but in case you missed it, it's Foster."

Then I looked at her again. The edges of her eyes were glittering. She dabbed angrily at them with her sleeve and then lifted her chin. "My name is Rachel." She looked at my outstretched hand with an expression of grim concentration before taking it with hers. I was surprised by her strong, sure grip even more than I was surprised by the callouses on her palm. “Rachel Walker.”

She said her name like it should mean something, but I just smiled and nodded. “It’s nice to meet you,” I said. And I really did mean it.

Chapter Thirteen

GABE

Even though I didn't want to, even though I wanted more than anything to stop, I still dragged my finger across the tablet, rewinding the video to the beginning again. The stupid blasting music, the white, italicized letters—how many of the millions of views this video had racked up were mine?

"I'm Gabe King and I'm the King of Pain!" the tiny, arrogant, *unbroken* version of me shouted into the camera. I hated his fucking guts, but the urge to punch the tablet screen had faded into a faint buzz in the back of my brain. I wasn't watching out of self-hatred anymore. I wasn't watching it punish myself. I was watching it out of...habit?

The thought made the corner of my mouth jerk into an unwanted smile, like someone had grabbed my lip with a fishhook. I coughed and then laughed, a dry mirthless sound, aware that sitting alone in my bedroom and chuckling to myself didn't exactly say much for my fraying, already suspect, sanity. Only *I* could make a habit of watching myself almost die. Only *I* could get bored of seeing my body broken and dashed against the rocks.

With a brand new wash of self-hatred, I nearly mustered the strength to turn it off. My finger hovered over the pause button, but I kept watching, transfixed right up to the moment the me on the screen leaped off that bridge.

"You're watching that again?"

I looked up, feeling as guilty as if I'd been caught with my hand down my pants. "What are you talking about?" I asked, trying to slowly drop the tablet out of his sight.

Beau shook his head as he walked into my bedroom. "The video. You've been watching it a lot."

"Stalker much?"

"Obvious much?" he countered. "You were always terrible at hiding things." A shadow crossed his face. "Hey, don't look at it anymore, okay?"

I hated the look of concern on his face because it was the same one he wore when he, Finn, and Claire had confronted me about my pill-addiction after the King Brothers imploded. The same wary sort of caution that you'd wear around a madman with a gun, or possibly a beloved family dog gone rabid. I never thought I'd make him have that look again, and I didn't want to think about what it meant he was thinking. So I tried for a lame attempt at humor. "Look at what?"

The concerned look stayed put. "You know what," he said, his voice so level you could use it to hang a picture on the wall.

Of course I wanted to protest that there was nothing wrong with what I was doing. Even though I could feel how wrong it was with every sweat-soaked, self-loathing viewing. I could feel it eating away at me. It was like climbing out of quicksand and then belly-flopping back in again for a second go-round. Willingly letting it suck me under. I glanced down at the tablet again. The video had ended, the white, italicized words scrolling by, letting the voyeuristic viewer know that Gabriel King survived his brush with death with two broken ankles, seven broken ribs, and a laceration on his side requiring twenty-two stitches to close and that filming of "King of Pain" was on hiatus, its fate uncertain. I sucked in a huge lungful of breath...

And then threw the tablet to the floor. "Take it," I told Beau.

His nostrils flared slightly. "Gabe, I'm not gonna fucking confiscate it from you like you're a bad little boy getting his toys taken away." He snorted. "Fuck, I'm not Claire." Then his eyes softened. "Just...be careful, okay?"

All at once my eyelids felt far too heavy to keep open anymore. "Take it," I urged. It was easier to talk with my eyes closed, easier to tell the truth without seeing him react to what I was saying. "I... I can't be careful, Beau. You know I don't know how."

His silence was more of a response than any words could have been.

"Take it," I pleaded with my eyes still closed.

"I've got it," he said.

I breathed a sigh of relief.

When I opened my eyes, Beau was no longer holding it. Whether he had shoved it up under his shirt, or quickly hidden it somewhere in the room, I had no idea. I didn't *want* to know. He knew I needed it gone right then and there.

Of course he did. He was Beau. "Now what are you going to do with yourself?" he asked me.

I stared at the ceiling. What I wanted to do was have Everly come over and give me another sponge bath, only this time she'd get in with me. I licked my lips, knowing full well that wasn't an answer Beau was going to want to hear and I was frustrated. "I dunno. Read a fucking book or something," I hissed. My eyelids were heavy again. I just wanted to sleep until Everly came over.

"Mom'll be happy to hear that," Beau said.

For a second I thought he had read my mind, until I realized he was talking about me reading a book. "Oh god no, don't tell her, she's gonna come home from work with an armload of books," I sighed. Beau was the type to sit there in a corner with a giant book in his lap, making frowny faces as he turned the page, but I'd never been able to sit still long enough for reading to work for me. "Oh god, and they're all gonna be about World War Two, I bet."

"Because you were interested in it."

"For like three months. In fifth grade."

Beau smiled. "Mom doesn't let go of things easily."

"Yeah, I know. She's still working at the library even though she and dad could have retired five times over by now. Especially with what we all gave them." A flicker of something crossed Beau's face. "What?" I asked.

"Nothing," Beau said, then kept talking. "You gave them a cut?"

"We all did," I said, narrowing my eyes. "We talked about this way back when."

"I know, and yeah, I gave them mine, and I'm pretty sure Jonah did his but..." he trailed off and I could see the internal fight. Loyalty to the family or loyalty to his twin.

Because I already knew what he was going to say. "Finn never gave his?" I asked, bristling.

Beau raised his hand to quiet me as he glanced at the door. "Mom and Dad don't know."

"How do they not..." I trailed off. "Oh."

Beau looked sheepish.

"You covered it for him," I sighed.

"It wasn't a big deal."

"What happened to his money?" I asked through clenched teeth. I still had most of my King Brothers money left in the bank and it wasn't like I'd been living a life of Spartan austerity these past few years. "How the fuck did he blow through..."

"He's gonna pay me back," Beau interrupted, waving his hand. "And it's not like I didn't have it either. I can't really think of a better use for my money than helping out my brother and my parents at the exact same time."

I mimed retching noises. He rolled his eyes. "Look, it's not like I didn't have enough to go out and get some toys."

"Toys. Now you're talking my language," I said. "What'd you get, an ATV? A jetski?"

"A fishing boat," Beau said proudly.

"What the fuck?" I breathed.

But he ignored me. "I take it up to Ganagua Lake in the summer. It's almost trout season too, so I have a few spots I want to hit. The creeks are all swollen with all this rain so it's not even safe to go out there in waders. You'd need a boat." His eyes got this faraway look. "Uncle Gid showed all his secret fishing places to me and Grandpa

King showed them to him. Like a family secret. I'll fish them someday with my kids."

This was a side of my younger brother I'd never seen before. "You want kids?"

He grinned. "A whole pack of 'em. Like us. Only smarter." He narrowed his eyes critically at me. "And better looking."

"They're gonna have to depend on their mom's genes for that, then."

He eyed the heavens and then gave me the finger as he stood up. "I'll take you out if you can promise not to be a gigantic prick about it."

"Thanks," I sighed. "I'm gonna need a new hobby soon enough."

He looked at me like I had three heads. "Why a new one? Your guitars are over in Dad's shed just gathering dust."

I swallowed. "Yeah, maybe," I said, trying to sound like I was thinking about it. But I wasn't. Ever since Noelle, the music that used to ring through my head at top volume fell silent. It was like losing a limb and I had no idea how to explain its loss to my brother who would undoubtedly tell me to just pick it up again and ignore how wrong it felt. I looked up at him, hoping that my expression was one of complete sincerity. "I'll do that, yeah."

Beau nodded. "In the meantime I'll have mom find you some books on the Battle of the Bulge."

"Oh god," I said, pinching the bridge of my nose with my thumb and forefinger. I could hear Beau's laughter ringing all the way down the stairs.

For a moment I closed my eyes in the silence he left behind, hoping for sleep to overtake me and rescue me from the restlessness that crawled under my skin. But after several long breaths I opened my eyes again. A nervous energy was coursing through me. I stood up carefully and hobbled to the window, then gazed out, earnestly scanning the trees, the omnipresent gray clouds, the rain-swollen creek like they were hiding something. I heard my pulse thudding in my temple and realized I was holding my breath and let it back out again.

She wasn't coming today.

She had her boards.

I knew this.

But the prospect of a whole day spent without her hard-won smile, without her unexpected laugh, made the day seem even bleaker than the gray clouds could. I missed her.

I fucking *missed* her.

Glancing at my phone, I counted the hours until she came over again. And then called myself pathetic. And then decided I couldn't get much more pathetic than a half-crippled shut-in standing by the window like a dog waiting for its master to return so why even bother caring? And then I gave myself the mental middle finger. I really was pathetic. I was even standing here imagining I could hear the sound of her terrible car starting, the coughing wheeze of an evil asthmatic, but that was stupid since there was no way I should recognize the sound of her car.

But I did. I was hearing it, and it didn't sound right. I felt the back of my neck prickle and before I knew it, I was strapping on my boots.

Chapter Fourteen

EVERLY

Every morning for the past month I awoke with the same breathless nightmare. That somehow I'd gotten the day wrong and slept through my alarm on the day of my boards.

But it never happened, and today? Today I awoke before my alarm, jerking out of a half-sleep and sitting straight up in my bed with a smile of anticipation.

It was today.

It was today!

And I was ready.

I flew down the stairs, the silent house a kind of blessing to my racing heart. I'd barely slept last night. When my breathing had finally slowed enough to let sleep creep in around the edges of my consciousness, my brain had taken over and started drilling me on questions. I dreamed half-formed dreams where I paged through my review books, the words dancing around on the pages, the sentences changing before I reached the end, and then jerked awake to check my phone alarm one more time.

I knew I must have fallen completely asleep at some point, because there had been a whole thing where it was Gabe King who was administering the exam, but then I snapped awake again before he took his shirt off to reveal that roadmap of scars.

I felt a flush, then shoved it from my mind. The last thing I could afford to be thinking about today was Gabe King.

I poured a cup of cold coffee left by my parents in the carafe and stuck it into the microwave. The seconds ticked down. My stomach roiled. I'd been prepping for this for four years and it was finally here. The misting rain hung in dreamlike curtains over the morning, adding to the sense that this wasn't exactly real. It hardly seemed possible that something I'd been looking forward to for so long was finally about to come true. My life was quiet and ordinary enough that there wasn't much I could say that about. I'd spent all those years crushing on Jonah and for what? He never noticed me. But he *had* put me in Gabe's line of sight.

The thought made me smile as I leaned against the stove and stared out the window. Gabe was up there in the King house, but I wasn't going to be seeing him today and for some reason that made me feel a tinge of melancholy. I wondered if it would be weird to go right over there after the boards were over. He'd probably want to hear how it all went. He didn't seem to mind talking to me, no matter how awkward I got. In fact, he seemed to actually enjoy himself, which meant that I enjoyed it too. I leaned in further, looking up the hill to the King house. His bedroom was on the north-facing side, which meant I couldn't see it, but that didn't stop me from craning my neck to maybe catch a glimpse of him hobbling past a window, hopefully wearing his boots like a good boy...

When the microwave beeped, I nearly jumped out of my skin. I grimaced as I pulled the hot mug out, feeling slightly ridiculous. Like the microwave had caught me and was disappointed by my daydreaming on today of all days.

I pushed all thoughts of Gabe from my brain and resolutely marched out the door. In all the mental rehearsals I had for this day, the sun had always been shining out full-strength and warm with encouragement. Instead it was another gray day of rain. It was the ninth straight day of rain and there was some talk about dangerous levels in the creek.

But that wasn't my concern right now. I got into The Grim Reaper and took a deep breath. "You and me today, kid," I said with a chuckle, and reached out to give the dashboard a fond pat.

Then I turned the key.

He coughed and then sputtered into silence.

I licked my lips. A faint tremor ghosted through my hands, and then I took a deep breath and laughed. "Oh, we're gonna be like that, are we?" I leaned back and cracked my knuckles. "Okay kid, you asked for it."

I turned the key.

He coughed.

Sputtered.

Then the engine caught and he roared to life. "Ha!" I crowed, smacking the steering wheel with the flat of my palm. "That's what I'm talking about!" I threw him into reverse and hit the gas.

He died.

For a moment he rolled silently until he ran out of momentum and ground to a halt, dead in the water.

Irritated, I threw on the E-brake and blew out an explosive sigh. The ghost of a tremor was back again, but if I gripped the steering wheel hard enough I didn't have to feel it. I took another deep breath and looked at the dash, gazing at it like I could somehow peer into my car's evil soul. "What the hell, Grim?" I asked him. "What is it? What did I do?"

There was no reply, of course, and thank heavens because then I'd know I really was cracking up. I sat for a moment, considering my next move. The engine was flooded, I could tell. I waited. The minutes ticked by and I tried to remind myself that I had plenty of time. I only needed fifteen minutes to get there. Add in another fifteen to find parking, walk in to the building, and take my seat and I was still a good twenty minutes early. I looked at the clock on my cell phone and breathed out and in as slowly as I could, trying to let my breath be the only thing I was concerned about. Forced meditation is still meditation, right?

After seven minutes I couldn't stand it any longer. "Okay, fucker," I told Grim. "Time to stop jerking me around like this."

I breathed a silent prayer and started the engine.

He coughed.

I swore and turned the key again.

The engine caught. Quickly, without taking time to showboat, I threw him into reverse again, and we rolled down the driveway together. "Yeah," I murmured quietly so he wouldn't hear me. I needed to get out onto the road immediately and hit the gas before he could sputter out again. I slowed at the end of the driveway to hastily check over my shoulder before pulling out onto my normally quiet country road.

There, up on the hill, a delivery truck was starting to trundle its way down.

I rolled to a stop and threw Grim into neutral, revving the accelerator to keep him from stalling again. "Come on," I begged the truck. It was too close for me to pull out now and the bridge was narrow enough that I wouldn't be able to squeeze past.

"Come on!" I shouted at the top of my lungs.

The truck blew by, rocking Grim like a baby in the cradle.

"Great," I said, baring my teeth in a determined smile. I backed out quickly and then threw Grim into drive before he got any bright ideas. I pressed the accelerator and started up the slight hill the truck had just come down. Five miles an hour. Ten miles an hour. The Kings' house slid slowly past me on my left.

Grim coughed again.

I scowled at the dash, shooting him a death glare that I hoped would scare him straight. He'd never done that while I was actually driving before. Only when I was starting up. "Settle down, Grim," I murmured. Fifteen miles an hour.

The whole car bucked like a horse in a rodeo. "What the—" I cried, throwing up my hands. Grim was jerking like a rocking horse. "Oh! No. No no no no no." One by one, every indicator on the dashboard was lighting up, like the streetlights in town winking on one after another at dusk. "No no no no no."

The engine fell silent and I slowly rolled backwards down the hill. Grim gave one last shudder.

And died for the last time.

Chapter Fifteen

GABE

When I heard the engine cut out fully, I grabbed my crutches and hauled myself down the hallway as fast as I could. "Beau!" I shouted. "Beau, you still here?"

My brother was MIA. I felt a flutter of helpless outrage, an impotent anger at how fucking helpless I was right now. Before my accident, I was fast enough, strong enough, to be out the door and checking on her already. But now I had to deal with these crutches and these stupid fucking boots when I just wanted to see that my girl was okay.

My girl.

I paused to let those words float in front of my brain for a moment before I batted them aside. Regardless of how I felt about her, I still had no idea how she felt about me. In between those flashes of warmth that made my face hurt from smiling, she was cool, detached, and skeptical. Her single-minded focus on her schooling seemed to leave no room for any distractions, and I was fairly certain that was how she viewed me—as a distraction. If I showed up right now, who knew if she'd accept my help. There was always the risk that she'd slap me in the face for invading her space.

What can I say? I like taking risks.

I placed the crutches carefully as I hopped down the stairs. She'd kick my ass if she knew I was doing this without help and for some reason that made me all the more determined to go find her and show her. "See? I can come find your ass, stop being a pain in mine."

There was no sound outside except the persistent patter of raindrops on the newly budded leaves. The rush of water in the creek was the loudest I had ever heard, loud enough even to drown out my ragged breath as I picked my way over the uneven terrain and down to the narrow bridge where I'd spotted her car. It sat there hulking like a shadow, the matte black exterior absorbing the light like a vehicular black hole. And next to it, standing stock still like she'd been frozen into place, was Everly.

She was slumped, fallen back against the side of the car, her face turned to the heavens in some kind of silent supplication. The rain was pattering relentlessly against her face, but she didn't seem to notice. She might even have been asleep, here in the middle of the road. But her eyes snapped open when she saw me drawing near.

I opened my mouth to greet her, but any snarky comment I wanted to say fled when I looked into her eyes. Those pretty eyes of hers, the ones that showed everything she thought she was hiding, looked completely lost. She was staring at me, glaring even, but there was no focus to them. She looked like she'd lost something she knew she'd never find again. "Everly?" I asked and it was a question I wasn't sure I wanted the answer to.

I expected her to burst into tears. I certainly thought she was about to by the way her eyes looked, opened wide and shining impossibly bright like that.

But she took a deep breath. She stumbled slightly—was she drunk?

And then I jumped because she started *laughing*. Full-on belly-laughing tinged with acute hysteria. I shuffled my crutches around to get closer to her and she stumbled again. I reflexively shot out my arm to catch her even though I was still shaky on my feet. She caught herself against it, bracing her feet and then slumping against the side of the car again in another fit of helpless, frightening laughter. "It died," she managed to gasp.

"What? Who died?" I demanded.

"It died today." She hiccuped and clapped her hand to her mouth, looking like she was about to vomit, then shook her head in wonder. "So many times it could have died," she breathed in a soft, helpless voice utterly unlike the one I was used to hearing come from her mouth. "But it chose today. Today..."

Goosebumps crawled across my rain-soaked skin. I was starting to feel genuinely freaked out. She lurched to the side again and this time I grabbed her and yanked her up, stumbling as I did so that we both fell against each other. Her eyes were wild now, looking everywhere but at me, and I could see her hands fluttering at her sides. Frustrated, I braced myself against my crutches and grabbed her face, turning her to me. "What happened?" I shouted, panicked now. "Are you okay?"

She couldn't seem to get a full breath. Gasping, she struggled to form words as tears slipped from her eyes and mixed with the rain on her cheeks.

I knew this. I had seen it in rehab. A panic attack. She was working herself up into a panic attack. Her eyes darted over my face and without really thinking about it, I reached down and grabbed her hand, holding it tight in mine. I cupped her cheek with my other hand then brushed it back, smoothing the fuzz of hairs that had escaped her no-nonsense ponytail.

Her eyes snapped to mine. I nodded. "That's it," I said. "Breathe when I breathe, okay? Slow down, just slow down, watch my face, okay? In and out. Slower. In and out. Okay? Good. Again. In and out. You're fine, Everly. You're safe and I'm right here."

"I can't," she moaned with each breath. "I can't, I can't..."

"You can. I'm here to help you, okay? I'm the nurse and you're the patient and I'm going to take care of you. In and out. You're doing so good." I smoothed her hair again and again, feeling the way her overheated skin was already cooling. "Good girl. You are doing so good, okay? Keep doing that. In and out."

Her bright blue eyes met mine and filled with tears. I smoothed her hair and smiled at her. "Hey there," I said. "You're back."

She reddened and her breath caught again. "No," I told her firmly. "Don't. Keep your breath nice and even. Don't try to talk yet."

She shook her head, but pressed her lips together dutifully and took another deep breath. "That's right." She looked down. The rain was caught in her dark lashes and fuck, why did she look so fucking beautiful to me right now? "Everly, come in out of the rain, okay?"

"My car," she started to say.

But I held up a hand. "My Dad's a car guy. You already knew that. If I text him and let him know there's a car stalled out in the middle of our road, he and his buddies will be out here and under the hood in no time flat. You don't have to worry about that. Just come inside and out of the rain, okay?"

I could see panic working its way back up into her eyes. "Let me help you," I urged.

"Why are you being so sweet to me?" she breathed, suspicion clouding her eyes.

"Because," I said. "I know what it's like."

She raised her eyebrows.

"Feeling like life is shitting on you for fun. Feeling like you can't catch a fucking break even though you're doing everything you're supposed to." And as I said it, I knew I was telling the truth. "We're kindred spirits."

She widened her eyes.

I laughed at her incredulous expression. "It's true. I know it doesn't seem like we have a thing in common, but we have everything important in common. Just look at me and tell me what happened. I can help you, Everly. Just tell me how to help you."

The cords in her neck stood out in sudden anguish. She took a deep breath and let out a sob. "I missed my boards!"

"Oh," I breathed. I felt like she'd punched me in the gut, so I couldn't even imagine how *she* was feeling. "Oh Jesus Christ, baby, I am so fucking sorry."

I didn't know what to do. She looked so fucking sad, so devastated and alone that it was tearing me up inside.

I did the only thing that felt right.

I kissed her.

It was an accident, I will swear it to my dying day. And hell, if you pressed me, I might even blather some nonsense about it being a friendly kiss, something to buck up her spirits after such terrible news.

It might have been an accident when I started kissing her, but continuing to kiss her was completely on purpose. Because there was something there, something that stirred a memory. Distant and fuzzy, as if half-remembered in a dream. It made no sense that I should "remember" kissing Everly. But when I felt it, I kissed her harder, hoping to jog that memory loose from where it was stuck in the back of my brain and make sense of it. And fuck, kissing her was pretty nice, too. Her lips were warm and soft and she tasted sweeter than made sense.

At first she held her mouth tightly closed. As I brushed my hand up to the back of her neck, her body was stiff and unyielding. The rush of desire I'd felt started to ebb when I felt how she wasn't into it, and the tendrils of memory started to slip through my fingers. I made to pull back and apologize, ready to let that memory slip past me as just some kind of weird deja vu.

Then she flung her arms around me and *fuck*, she kissed me back.

For all of her tightly held emotions, she kissed with a wild desperation. She was like a hungry animal the way she devoured my mouth and battled my tongue with hers. I was shocked, and then I was more turned on than I ever had been in my life to feel her coming alive under my hands.

She sought under my shirt, seeking warm skin. I tilted her head, devouring that soft, amazingly hot mouth as the memory came back with a vengeance, burning through all my synapses until I pulled back and stared at her, feeling like I'd been hit by a truck. "You," I gasped, cupping her face in my hands and searching those blue eyes. "Oh my god, you're her. It was you!"

Chapter Sixteen

EVERLY

Gabe tasted the same as he had that stolen night I'd been trying to forget since I started working for the Kings.

The jolt of surprise memory was enough to silence the stream of panic. His hands on my face were strong enough to hold me together long enough for me to catch my breath and gasp in surprise.

So much adrenaline pumped through my veins that I rose up on my toes and flung myself against his chest, desperate to hold on to something. I was ready to fall. I gasped again when he caught me.

He groaned in response to my gasp and suddenly his tongue was sliding against mine and goddamn, *yes*, I did remember this. The way he kissed. The way he didn't hold back. Usually I was the one to hold back, but I had no strength left to keep up my defenses.

He was the one to draw back. Jerked back, more like. "Did I hurt you?" I wanted to ask, mindful of his injuries even with my clouded brain.

"Oh my god, you're her," he said.

I exhaled sharply. My heart stalled in my chest.

"It was you!" he exclaimed, gripping my shoulders and giving me a little shake.

I jerked. Stiffened in his arms and drew back, staring at his opened mouth. He looked at me like I was a stranger, and in that moment I understood that he didn't know me, because I didn't even know myself. I'd been convinced he didn't remember. I'd been certain that that night was one both of us had let slip through our fingers.

His eyes widened. "It was you," he repeated, his voice harsher now. An accusation. "You never...how?"

I swallowed and closed my eyes, partly to escape the way his soft hazel eyes had gone intense green with emotion. And partly to remember.

I still remembered every single detail of that night in December. And even though I was in Gabe's arms, I was right back there on the barstool, sitting close to the door. Watching the party but not taking part in it.

I was humming.

It was a bad habit. Left over from when I was a bespectacled nobody at Crown Creek Primary and the laughter and chatter went on around me like I wasn't there. I'd hum to be part of the noise. To be included.

That night I'd hummed into my rum and coke as I drank it way too quickly. The sugar made my lips sticky so I kept licking them as I glanced at the door again and again. The caffeine in the coke made my head buzz and my hands were starting to shake on their own.

I wasn't supposed to be out. I was scared about the unit test the next week, a unit test that ended up being cancelled because of a huge snow storm that hit the area, dumping thirty-three inches in thirty-six hours. That night I hadn't known that. I only knew that being in the bar felt like a major transgression.

But when I'd seen the flyer on campus, my heart had stalled in my chest. I stared at it, even brushed my fingers over it to make sure it was real.

Jonah was playing. Right here in his hometown. I'd always been a fan, but I'd never been able to see him play, not solo, not even with his brothers. Now that he was this huge, massive star, the likelihood of me being able to see him, being able to afford the tickets to get close enough, was slim to none. Except he was back in town and playing a show at the Crown Tavern. The flyer said so.

I'd promised myself that I'd study early the next morning. Then I'd shown up super early and claimed a bar stool, determined not to miss the chance to have Jonah King finally notice me.

I was there so early that I noticed every single person who walked in after me. People I recognized from around town and people I didn't, even though I knew I should.

I was there when the rest of the King Brothers showed up, three of the four of them. I ducked into my rum and coke and felt them file past rather than watch them waving to the crowd like the local heroes they were. Scowling Finn, solemn Beau...

And smiling Gabe.

I remembered the smile, and more than that, I remembered the smile making me angry. Back when the brothers played together, there was a rivalry that was implied if never actually spoken. If you were a Jonah fan, you did not trust Gabe, and the feeling was mutual. There were message board clashes and I'd heard of fights breaking out at shows. Of course I'd grown up enough to see that was silly, but some deeply ingrained part of me, the obsessive fan that would never fully die, still held on to that anger. His smiling face, his deep laugh, his easy way with the townspeople who asked for autographs—they weren't plusses in my book. They were all reasons to sneer.

Even as I felt those feelings, I was horrified by them. That the fangirl hive-mind was still controlling me was shocking. I'd always considered myself a rational girl who had her feet firmly on the ground. I had no actual reason to hate Gabe King, but I also knew I wasn't there to see him. I was there for his brother.

I looked at the door again.

No Jonah.

Where was he?

People filled in the spaces around me. After nearly two hours of solitude, my space was overflowing with elbows and "excuse mes." I held my ground. I was a rock in the middle of a fast-flowing river, clutching my drink possessively. Whether it was my third or my fourth by then, I couldn't recall. The rum hit my bloodstream hard. I leaned back on the barstool, needing something to prop myself up on. The woodgrain was cool under my fingers.

A gust of wind sent the front door slamming into the outside wall, and that was what started it all.

"Holy shit. It's getting bad out there." A voice at my side.

I'd turned, smiling, but the person was talking to someone over my head. There was a shout of laughter. Bodies jostled together. I felt warm and eager and happy and I wanted to be a part of it. I'd looked around, wanting to make eye contact with someone. I searched the room for someone to smile at and my eyes slid right onto Gabriel King's face.

He was looking at me. Squinting, like he was trying to place me. I'd grown up next door to him, but this was the first time we were face to face in years. In the whole of the bar, he was the first person to look at me and notice I was there. The corner of his mouth turned up in a lazy half-smile.

The corner of my mouth tugged upward as he held my gaze. I wanted to believe it was the rum heating my cheeks like that. He was the wrong brother. That same indignant anger twisted in my belly, but it felt less like a reaction and more like a reflex because I liked smiling at him. And I liked the way he was looking at me, like I was something worth memorizing. I had dolled myself up for Jonah, but I wasn't so un-girly not to hope that Gabe was noticing my seldom-worn makeup or the careful way I'd curled my hair. Or the way my new bra—not a sports bra, a real bra—made me look in my tank top. I'd barely recognized myself when I looked in the mirror before leaving, but it was worth it to see the other side of his mouth turn up. He'd lifted his chin then, a silent invitation.

But he was the wrong brother. I had to remember that.

With some difficulty I'd turned back to the door as a shout went up. It sounded like a fight was about to break out and I drunkenly mustered my training, wondering if I'd be called upon to nurse any head wounds tonight.

Gabe's voice rose above the shouts. "Drinks are on me!" he'd called, and everyone started cheering.

Another rum and coke appeared and I was drunk enough to lunge at it and guzzle it down. It felt like I was moving even though I was sitting perfectly still. I hummed aloud, not worrying if anyone heard me. I smiled to myself and broke out laughing when someone next to me told a joke. My veins fizzed and my face hurt from smiling. Why didn't I do this more often? Why wasn't I a normal girl who went out and drank and laughed and had fun? Why couldn't I be a person who did these things? Why couldn't I have the guts to cut loose once in a while?

I wanted desperately to be the kind of girl that this night would come easily to. I'd come out to see Jonah and he still hadn't shown up. I wanted to not read into that. I wanted to believe there was a simple explanation for why he was late to his one-night-only, special-for-the-town performance, and not that I had somehow fucked up.

And just like that, I flipped from pleasantly drunk to something much darker. Paranoia licked at the edges of my mind, insisting that this, all of this, this whole night was just an elaborate trick. That the same tormentors who had hounded me growing up had organized this to mock me. That everyone here was pretending, and they'd all start laughing.

I took a deep sip of my drink. No. That was insane. I wasn't insane. I was a regular girl who sometimes got really nervous about silly things. Silly. It was all silly. There was a reason Jonah was over an hour late and it had nothing to do with me. He probably got in an accident and was lying in a ditch somewhere. The roads had gotten super bad since I'd come here hours ago.

But the idea of Jonah King in an accident was completely foreign to me. He was invincible. Untouchable. That couldn't be it. No, there was some other reason. Was Gabe worried too? I turned and tried to find him in the ever-thickening crowd. I could see the sandy brown of his hair but I couldn't see his face because he'd been swallowed up by the revelers. "Jesus, where is he?" came a loud, drunk voice.

"Probably fucking his girl," I heard the bartender snarl.

I froze.

Jonah? Was he talking about Jonah?

More voices joined the conversation. I strained my ears to listen in. I even stopped humming.

"He's dating that girl," someone else explained. "What's her name? The kindergarten teacher."

"Ruby Riley?" came the reply. "Oh, I like her. She's sweet."

My stomach dropped to my toes.

Jonah was dating a local girl.

I knew he'd never end up with me. I'd always known I was too ordinary. Too literally the girl next door. But if he wasn't going to be with me, I always hoped he'd be with some glamorous Hollywood Amazon. Some kind of otherworldly modelesque creature with high cheekbones and a smile that didn't show so much gum. Not Ruby. I'd met Ruby. Though I doubted she'd remember me, I knew her.

She was one of the nice ones. A nice normal girl. Which was something I knew that I would never be.

I'd stood up with my heart pounding, intent on fleeing, but when I stood the sudden sway of the floor under my feet showed me how drunk I was. There was a burst of laughter when someone cut the sound on the sedate Christmas music that had been playing in the background and plugged in an old King Brothers song. I was suddenly enveloped in a sea of dancing bodies, my own body swaying to its own internal rhythm as I looked around, wide-eyed as Jonah's recorded voice came on through the loud speaker.

Gabe was watching me again.

The sound of the right brother's voice crooning to me as the wrong brother looked me up and down was too much. Something inside of me squeezed tight and fell away. I started moving to him.

Him.

The wrong brother.

The crowd parted like the Red Sea and I walked right up to him. "Hey." It was all my tongue could manage.

He grinned that grin that started at one side of his mouth and spread across his whole face. I'd seen that grin so many times since then, but that night was the first time he'd let me experience it. It was like getting hugged by a smile. That night, his hazel eyes looked the exact same shade as his brother's. That's why I could pretend he was Jonah.

I told myself that's why I went to him, because I wanted to pretend he was his brother. I'd repeated that lie to myself many, many times after that night, but now I was finally realizing what I was pretty sure

I'd known all along. It was a lie. I'd gone to Gabe believing that I wanted him to be like Jonah. But Jonah had never noticed me.

Gabe had.

He'd grinned when he looked down at me. Maybe he was amused by how I was swaying to the music, the rum making my limbs floppy and my movements fluid. At some point, he must have put his hand on my waist but when I finally noticed the warmth of his fingers, they'd felt like they'd been there forever. I leaned in to the pressure of it, liking the way he was holding me up.

We danced. Jonah's voice filled my ears, but Gabe was filling every one of my other senses.

"I shouldn't have come out tonight!" I'd said. I wanted to hate myself now that I knew that there was no chance of catching Jonah's eye that night, but it was hard to hate anything when I was swaying in Gabe's arms. I tried to imagine Jonah holding me like this, but that wasn't real. This was.

"I have to study," I finished lamely, dredging up another reason to hate myself when I was feeling so damn good.

He grinned again, and the last bit of hatred fell away. This was how it could happen. This was how I could be a normal girl. Swaying to the music with Gabe's hands at my waist and his eyes on my face. I realized my eyes were half-slitted and opened them wide to peer up—way up—at him.

Was his face always that close? I was staring at him, I knew it, but there was no way to stop myself. I'd never been this close to his face before, and even though it was so familiar, there were still things to discover. Like how his eyes actually had way more green in them than Jonah's did. I liked them. I also liked the way his chest felt under my hands. Warm and real. I liked how he leaned down and rested his forehead against mine. "I feel like I should know your name," he said. "We've met before, right?"

"Yeah." I tossed my head, laughing. It was the rum that was making this so amusing. "A bunch of times."

"Really?" He looked distressed. "I would have remembered you."

This should have bothered me but it didn't. If he didn't know me, then I was free to be whoever I wanted. And I wanted to be the girl I was right now, with him. In the whole bar, he'd only danced with me. He was the wrong King Brother, but he felt pretty damn right under my hands. Real, while his brother was a fantasy. I was drunk and I wasn't going to remember this in the morning. I wasn't *me* tonight, so I did what I thought a regular girl would do.

"Kiss me!" I demanded, wrapping my arms around his neck and shouting up to him.

He looked confused, but not disgusted. "What?" he said, but I could tell by the twinkle in his eye that he had heard me.

I pulled him down and pressed my lips to his.

Everything went black.

The music cut out as the lights went dark and everyone started screaming. The power had gone out and everyone went crazy, bumping into each other in the pitch dark, but the only thing I cared about was how Gabe's lips felt on mine and how good it felt when he kissed me.

I'd been the one to yank him down and press my mouth to his, but *he* was the one who was kissing *me*.

And holy hell could he kiss.

Everything slowed down. Time was like taffy getting stretched and pulled so that moments stretched out into infinity and I noticed every detail even as the rum made everything distorted. I knew his hands couldn't really be everywhere at once, but that's what it felt like. One hand ran through my hair as the other pressed against my back and still there was his hand caressing my face, tilting my head to deepen the kiss. In the darkness I swore I saw sparks but whether they were in the air or behind my eyes I couldn't tell.

It was the darkness that made this okay. In the darkness I could pretend I was someone else.

He made a sound in his throat, the kind of sound I'd never heard before but somehow my body knew to respond to. I arched into him, and the way my nipples ached as they pressed into his hard chest made me moan into his mouth. He answered my moan by sliding his fingers into my hair and tugging slightly, messing up my careful curls in a way I welcomed. I wanted to feel him tugging gently as he tilted my head back. I wanted his hand wandering down my side, brushing lightly but firmly against the side of my breast. I pressed into him, sliding my hands down his arms to feel the strength under his skin and he growled something into my neck. In the dark, people were bumping into us, jostling as they shouted for friends and yelled about the lights, but I couldn't see anyone. The darkness was thick and total, which was why I let his lips wander down my neck.

Every nerve in my body sang. I dug my toes into the soles of my shoes as his lips brushed up against my earlobe. I moaned and arched again and I heard his murmuring laugh and felt his thigh nudge its way between my legs. I gasped and moaned again as he pressed it upward, and he covered my mouth and swallowed my panting with a kiss as he snaked his hands down to my hips and pulled me firmly against his thigh.

My singing taut nerves frayed and I fell against him, gasping in disbelief at what was happening. A searing heat clawed its way through my core. My breath caught and I knew that I was seconds away from having an orgasm right there in the dark, just from the press of his thigh. It didn't help that he cursed and murmured into my ear as my breath quickened. I turned my head up to stare at him, even though I couldn't see him, and with some kind of sixth sense he found my mouth again.

A sudden red glow illuminated everything, like we'd wandered into a bordello.

"Backup generator's on!" came the shout, and there they were, everyone around us in the red glow of the exit lights.

I stepped back and out of Gabe's hands. His eyes were still closed, like he hadn't realized I wasn't kissing him anymore. A soft smile was on his face. He looked...fucking beautiful, different and brand new to me. Something reached into my chest and squeezed my heart so tight I gasped.

He must've heard me, because he half-opened his eyes and the mortification of what I'd done flooded in. I was shocked at what I'd allowed to happen between us—the intimacy, the pleasure—and all because I'd wanted to pretend he was his brother. It was wrong. This was so wrong.

I wasn't this kind of girl at all. I couldn't do this. Not to myself, and not to him.

Before his eyes had opened fully, I turned and fled. I ran for the door and pushed it open, pushing hard against the whipping wind and driving snow.

I thought I heard him shout when the door slammed. But how could he call for me if he didn't know my name? If he had no idea who I was, then it could be like it had never happened at all.

But it had happened. And now, somehow, it was happening again.

"It was you." It wasn't a question he was asking. It was a statement. He wasn't unsure, he knew.

I let my fingers trail over his good arm and closed my eyes. I licked my lips. "It was me," I confessed, and it was like the floodgates opened in my chest. A tightness I hadn't known was there loosened and I gulped in my first full breath since I'd started working as his nurse.

"Why didn't you tell me?" he asked, looking wounded and excited at the same time.

That night I'd wanted to pretend he was his brother, but now all I wanted was him. "I didn't think you remembered, and I didn't want things to get...weird."

"But *you* remembered."

I blinked. "Of course."

He opened his eyes wide. For a moment I thought he might start yelling. I would have deserved it. By not telling him, I'd been lying all this while, and he'd have every right to be pissed about it.

But then his smile, that slow, lazy smile that split his whole face into a manic grin, spread across his face. "Holy shit." He brushed his hands up my arms, as if wanting to be sure I was real. "You looked so *different* that night." He squinted. "But now I see it. Your eyes...fuck, I should have known you from the eyes, but..."

"But it was dark," I said with a small laugh. The leftover adrenaline from my panic attack ebbed away, making me sleepy and sated. "It was dark pretty much the whole time."

Chapter Seventeen

GABE

The night I'd kissed Everly without knowing her name was also the night my brother almost died.

I hadn't known until much later that the reason Jonah was so late for his show was that he and Ruby had gone off the road in the storm. They'd gotten trapped in her car without a cell phone and nearly succumbed to hypothermia before Jonah dragged them through the whiteout to a farmhouse to call for help. He had the scars from frostbite on his fingers to remember that night for the rest of his life, but I'd only had a kiss in the dark.

I'd been pissed at my brother for being so late. I'd had to quell the crowd's increasing agitation by buying a round for the whole bar. My younger brothers both gave me the eye when I did this, but I gave them the finger. It wasn't like *I* was drinking. It was Cokes for me forevermore.

The news traveled through the bar fast and everyone was happy again. The sweet thump of triumphant adrenaline dumped into my veins, that buzzy high of risk-taking the only high I could chase now. In an instant I'd turned the mood from near riot to full-on party.

Jonah owed me, I'd thought.

I glanced toward the front door again.

And that's when I saw *her*.

There at the corner, perched on a stool with her whole body tense, was a girl who looked so familiar that I'd done a double take. The way the light shone down on her made her look like she was bathed in a spotlight. Her curly blonde hair fell like a waterfall down her back, with a few shorter tendrils sweeping down to graze her creamy cheeks. Her hair and eyes were all softness but there was a hard edge to her mouth that I liked. A lot. "Who is that?" I leaned in and asked my brother.

"Who?"

"The girl! On the stool by the door?"

Beau looked over as she slid from her stool and melted into the crowd. "What girl?"

"Forget it." I was still looking at where she was, at the negative space she left there at the very edge of the bar.

Beau watched me watch for her. "You're actually paying attention to a girl?" I glared at him. He raised his eyebrows innocently. "What?"

"Don't start."

He grumbled and headed over to the bar with his twin and Claire, all of them refilling their beers on my dime and leaving me alone.

"Hey."

I turned and there she was, right in front of me, a strangely purposeful expression on her face. "Hi," I said, because what else is there to say when the first girl to catch your eye in nearly two years is talking to you? I winced at how rusty I'd grown.

I stepped to her. I wasn't drunk, but I felt like it. She laughed, a wild sound. What's so funny? I wondered.

"I usually don't come out," she said, shaking her head. She rocked on her heels, bumping lightly against me.

I reached out to steady her and liked the way she felt under my hand. Her skin was really soft. "I feel like I should know your name. We've met before, right?"

She'd tossed her head and laughed like this was the most amusing thing she'd ever heard. "Yeah, a bunch of times."

I knew it. I knew she was right. There was something about her, but I couldn't place her at all and it was pissing me off because I wanted to know her. I wanted to know everything about her. "I would have remembered you," I told her, because I would have sworn it was true.

She'd gotten this wild look in her eyes that made me want to press her against the wall and make her scream my name.

She looked at me like she could read my thoughts. I loved the way her eyes were shining at me. I could get addicted to having her look at me like that. I was an addict, after all.

The storm howled outside. Cold air seeped in through the window but she was warm and without discussing it, we started moving, dancing to the cheesy Christmas music piped in through the speakers. I didn't care about the music. I wasn't sure why she was in my arms, but it felt right to have her there, just like it felt right to bend and kiss her after only a moment.

"Kiss me," she said.

I couldn't believe my luck. "What?" I had to be sure that's what she really wanted because I was ready to do all that and more.

Our lips connected.

Everything went black.

The darkness was total. Silently I thanked Jonah for being a prick and missing his own concert, because this was way better than any show of his could be. I kissed her with two years' worth of pent up emotions, all the things I'd bottled up inside and only let out when I jumped out of airplanes or rode dirt bikes on the dunes in the Sahara. Kissing this familiar stranger was the same kind of adrenaline rush.

Bodies thumped and jostled us, rocking us like a boat on ocean waves. I'd only seen her for a second, but sight didn't seem important right now. What was important was the way she felt in my arms, the smell of her shampoo as I buried my nose in her hair. Her voice, low and husky, was what mattered. The taste of her lips was the most important thing about her.

It felt like seconds, but it was also as long as a lifetime.

The generator kicked in and the emergency lights came on. I blinked as my eyes adjusted, and in the whooping crush of people surging together in celebration, she slipped from my grasp. "Hey!" I growled, shoving a guy to the side. "Watch out for the lady!"

He glanced at me, eyes unfocused. "What lady?"

I turned. "Hey!" I called. "Where'd you go?"

I caught a flash of blonde hair. A bright streak of red lip. Was that her? "Baby?" I didn't even know her fucking name. I spun around, my heart racing. "Hey ,wait a fucking minute! Let me get your number at least?"

A rush of cold air. "Close the goddamned door!" someone shouted.

"Wait, no. Don't!" I shoved my way through everyone in Crown Creek, all these people here to see my brother. I had found the one thing for me, the first girl to stir anything in my soul since I'd caught Noelle. I knew, with a certainty I seldom felt, that if I found her again, I wouldn't have to keep doing what I'd been doing. Pushing myself. Running on empty. Risking everything. I knew that if I caught up to her, she'd help me learn to stay still.

The door slammed shut, caught by the wind. The shuddering reverberation went right down to my toes. It felt *final*, but no, fuck that. I pushed it back open.

Freezing cold air bit into my bare forearms. The temperature had plummeted at least fifteen degrees since I'd left the house. It was the kind of startling cold that took your breath away, but that wasn't why I swore under my breath.

There was nothing in the road. Caught in the streetlight, the falling snow swirled in a storm of glitter, like the finale of one of our shows. The snow was all I saw.

The wind was already scouring her footprints off the sidewalk. In the distance there was the glow of brake lights as the only car on the road turned out of sight.

She was gone.

I knew her lips. I knew her shape. I could still taste her kiss.

But I didn't know who she was, why she was so familiar. The suffocating familiarity of my hometown fell away, leaving me like I was an alien, a stranger dropped in an unfamiliar place where I didn't know the language.

But her body was still etched into my skin. If I touched her again, I would know her. I only had to find her again.

But I didn't know her name.

Until now.

"Everly," I repeated, and kissed her again.

Chapter Eighteen

GABE

I was at physical therapy. That fact alone was usually enough to put me in a bleak frame of mind.

But today I was happy for reasons I couldn't quite explain.

"You're in a good mood today!" Kristyn trilled as she manipulated my ankle.

I glanced up at Everly. Only a few days had passed since we found each other again, but everything had changed. I'd found her. I'd found her, and she'd been right under my nose all along.

Her blue eyes were fixed on my foot with a look of extreme concern on her face. Her lips were screwed up in sympathy as she watched Kristyn go through the exercises.

Her lips.

They were all the explanation my happiness needed. It didn't even matter that it felt like Kristyn was driving knives into my feet. I'd found the girl. My lost girl from my lost night.

For the first time in a long time I felt like things were starting to go my way. I felt like I was floating on a cloud. Hell, I felt like I was high, but this was one hundred percent natural. Real, honest-to-god happiness.

I'd forgotten what that felt like.

Kristyn hopped back up to her feet. "Can you stand up, please?" she asked, gesturing to the floor.

"'Course I can," I said. I could fucking do anything. I leaped off the table.

"Whoa, slow down," she warned, holding up her hands.

I grinned and waved away her concern. "I'm fine. I've never felt better. Watch!" I stood up. "See that?" I straightened my back, stretching up to my full height for the first time in months. I glanced over at Everly, who was watching me, unable to hide her smile. "Come here," I told her.

She wrinkled her nose but got up anyway. "You're not overdoing it right now, are you?" she asked, then looked at Kristyn. "Is he?"

Kristyn made scales of her hands, weighing one side, then the other. "It's really up to him."

"Yeah, baby, it's really up to me," I said with a wink. She rolled her eyes and I reached out and pulled her in to me. "I bet you had no idea how tall I actually am," I said with a smirk.

She lifted her chin. "I knew exactly how tall you were," she said in a voice so heavy with meaning I felt my cock jump. And one more time I was reminded that she was it. She was the girl I'd kissed. And more than that, she seemed to enjoy kissing the new Gabe as much as she'd enjoyed kissing the old one.

The new Gabe kissed her right there on the therapy floor.

She kept her mouth firmly closed—ever the professional—but her lips were soft and yielding. I brushed my good hand up to her hair and she gently extricated herself from my grasp with a firm, "Therapy time."

"I'm totally cured now," I told her. "That was all it took." I touched her lips with my fingers.

She rolled her eyes again.

I laughed. "No, it's true. Want to see?" I trotted in a tight circle around her. "I can run circles around you now," I said with a wicked grin.

"Oh my god. You're terrible at puns."

"You mean amazing."

Her eyes shone and she glanced sheepishly in Kristyn's direction before confessing in a whisper, "I love puns."

I wanted to kiss her again, but right then Kristyn cleared her throat. "Gabe! Why don't we go over and do some stair steps now?"

"Can I walk over there?" I asked.

Kristyn made those weighing scales again. "Stop if you feel pain."

I started walking, reveling in how straight and strong my body felt. I was so fucking thrilled that I didn't say anything when something tweaked in my right ankle. I didn't even miss a step.

"Ten reps on each side. I want you to plant your entire foot, not just the ball of it," Kristyn ordered.

"Look," I called out, wanting Everly's eyes on me again. "I'm Jane Fonda. Jazzercise. Ready?" I clapped my hands in a four count, then shouted, "Grapevine!"

"You're a nut. You're gonna fall!" she shouted.

"I am not," I declared, even as my foot came down wrong. I stepped back, landing hard on my heel as I tried not to lose my balance. The shock of the landing reverberated right up my newly healed leg. An involuntary yelp escaped my mouth as my still-weak ankle turned with a sharp, searing pain. In a last-ditch effort to save myself, I crossed my other foot over and planted it, gritting my teeth as the same jolting shock raced up my other leg.

Kristyn reached out to catch me, and Everly was a mere second behind in grabbing my other arm. Shame made me press my lips together and say nothing when Everly asked if I was okay. I also kept my mouth shut when Kristyn asked if I needed any ice, just shaking my head. My ankles were screaming and inside of my head I was screaming right along with them. Because just like that, all of the pain that I thought happiness had washed away came flooding right back.

Chapter Nineteen

EVERLY

Even though it was gray and awful outside, I felt like I had my own personal sun shining inside of my chest.

Every time I looked at Gabe, I felt that warmth again. Every time he smiled at me with that giddy smile, like we were sharing an incredible secret that no one else was privy to, I felt that sun's brilliance. It shone into all of the dark corners of my mind and warmed all the frozen places in my chest.

The sun was inside of me, but it also seemed to shine on me too. Every time Gabe looked at me, I felt like I was stepping out of the shadows to be seen for the first time. It was a new and strange feeling to be *seen* this way and it made me feel like everything I did was significant, like time was stretching out so that every second was important.

I'd tried to act normal, but nothing felt normal any more.

Normal would have been him getting super pissed at me for keeping my identity secret for so long. Normal would have meant that he wouldn't have remembered at all, or, worse, he would have but it hadn't meant a damn thing to him.

He hadn't done any of that. He'd just touched my face as relief crossed his and then he'd laughed with wild delight.

And then he'd kissed me again.

Was this my new normal? I wondered as I sat in the therapy room, watching Gabe as he did his exercises and trying to keep the fawning smile off my face. Was my new normal just...spending time with this guy who made me so damn happy?

He'd kissed me this morning when I came to pick him up, a long, deep kiss that made my blood sing. I'd never felt like this before. My whole life I'd held myself separate, but now I was so connected to a person. I felt like a thin cord had been stretched between our bodies, allowing me to feel what he felt. And what he felt—felt for *me*...

Let's just say it was making it super hard to be a professional.

Professional nurses don't kiss their patients in the middle of therapy sessions. They especially don't do this when other professionals are right there watching with dumbstruck looks on their faces. I could feel Kristyn's disbelief when Gabe pressed his lips to mine, and that was the only thing that kept me from throwing my arms around him and letting him devour my mouth like he wanted to.

But I still let his lips linger there on mine a whole lot longer than I should have before I finally remembered I was a nurse.

Reddening, I drew back from him and tugged at my shirt. I tried to put some distance between us, both physical distance and emotional, as I reminded myself that, regardless of the fact that I'd missed my boards, I still had a professional reputation to maintain.

But that thin cord of connection wouldn't let me have distance. I felt Gabe's disappointment when I pulled away—felt it so acutely, even, that I smiled at him reassuringly.

Which Gabe—being Gabe—took as an invitation to start overdoing it.

"Are you okay?" I gasped, rushing to his side as he stumbled off the stairstep.

He didn't say anything. I didn't know him well enough to know if this was a good thing or a bad thing. "Do you need some ice?" Kristyn asked.

Still, nothing. I studied his face. That connection told me that his pride had been wounded. "Let's head out," I told him, keeping my tone light and encouraging. Professional, even. "You worked really hard today. I'm impressed."

He glanced at me. I smiled and nodded but when he didn't smile back, the sun in my chest dimmed a little. Confused, I hurried around the therapy room to fetch all of our things. I grabbed him his crutches and waited for his grateful smile.

With his head down, he sneered at the floor and snatched them from my hands, every inch the arrogant celebrity rockstar he had been most of his life.

I was stung, but I lifted my chin anyway. "You good?"

"Fine," he said curtly. His mouth was still drawn up in a sneer.

I pressed my lips together and opened the door. He hopped through, not even saying thank you. My trained eye went right to his ankles, noting that he was moving a lot more gingerly leaving therapy than he had been when we arrived. "You hurt yourself back there," I stated flatly. It wasn't a question.

"I'm fine," he said, reaching for the door.

"Are you kidding?" I snapped, rushing around to grab the door handle from him. His stubbornness was getting under my skin. "You're supposed to let me get that."

"I don't need your help," he said, blowing past me and heading to his mom's SUV. We'd borrowed it to get to the session since Grim was still being treated by his dad.

I should have let it go. I should have let it roll off of me like I'd done so many times before. But that light in my chest had started shining—shining because of him—and now the darkness wasn't acceptable anymore.

I hurried after him. He stopped when I clapped my hand on his shoulder, but he didn't turn around. "You do need my help," I reminded him. "You're hurt. It's okay to take help when you're hurt."

His shoulder rose on an inhale like he was about to say something, but he just shook his sandy head and kept hopping to the car.

I stood there frozen for a moment, stunned by his coldness. I had this desperate urge to turn on my heel and walk away from him, to leave and refuse to be treated this way by the rockstar version of Dr. Jekyll and Mr. Hyde.

But I was his nurse.

So I took a deep breath and got into the driver's seat next to him.

The silent ride home was the exact opposite of the warm, teasing ride there. At the stoplight at Four Corners, I hazarded one quick glance at him. He was turned away and staring out the window into the gray drizzle. His jaw was tense and his eyes were narrowed. Was I seeing anger or pain? That connection between us seemed to have broken, leaving me adrift.

The next day was no different. He grunted answers to my questions and refused to stand to make it easier for me to check his dressing. "How's your pain level?" I asked pointedly, unable—no, unwilling—to stand his silence any longer.

"I'm fine," he grunted, but pain was written all over his face.

I wanted to reach for him, but he pulled back when he saw my hand rise. I let it fall back down to my side, then silently gathered my things and left his house. My lips ached for his kiss, my body craved his embrace, and I tried to remind myself what normal was for me. In reality nothing had changed.

Except *I* had.

And when the silent treatment stretched out into its fourth day, I'd had enough. "You're in pain," I told him as I helped him into his shirt.

He wasn't meeting my eyes, but I could tell by the set of his jaw that he'd heard me.

"It's time you stop messing around with the ibuprofen." There was a note of pleading in my voice and I cleared my throat in an futile attempt to get rid of it. *Just kiss me again*, my brain was screaming, but my pride insisted I be angry with him rather than beg. "I know you have prescriptions for stronger pain relief. Stop being stubborn and take them!"

His eyes flicked to me, the first time he'd looked me in the eye in days, and the pure fury in them made me step back. He blinked and it was gone, replaced with that stubborn gleam. "I'm fine," he said, but at least this time he was saying it to me rather than at me.

I shook my head. "You're not yourself."

"You'd know that, huh?" he shot back.

I opened my mouth, closed it, and stepped back grimly. "Fair point," I said, trying to keep the hurt from my voice. "How about I ask Jonah if he thinks you're fine?" He glared at me and I lifted my chin in challenge. *Yeah, didn't think of that, huh?* "Or Beau." I added. "Is he gonna agree that you're fine?"

He eyed me slowly, letting his gaze drop down to my body before flicking back up to my face. "You can go," he finally said.

The utter dismissal in his voice was so abrupt that it extinguished the last hopeful light inside of me as efficiently as snuffing out a candle flame. "You're firing me?"

"I didn't say that."

"You pretty much did."

"I'm just saying I don't need your help today." He looked away.

I took a step back...

And then shook my head. "Hell no," I snarled. "You need my help every day. That's why your family hired me. To take care of you."

"I didn't want them to," he said.

"Liar."

"You're calling me a liar?"

"Yup. Right to your face." I stepped forward again. "Liar."

"I don't need your help!"

"Yeah?" I challenged. "Go on," I said, gesturing to the floor. "Stand up on your own then."

He glared at me. He didn't rise to his feet the way he'd been able to do before that disaster of a therapy session. "Right," I said, crossing my arms. "It's time to stop acting like a spoiled brat and take those painkillers."

"It's time to stop acting like a bitch and get out of here," he snapped, eyes blazing.

I stepped back and pressed my hands to my belly, where I would have sworn he'd plunged a knife. "Did you really just say that?"

"Jesus Christ, Everly," he said with a heavy sigh. He looked to the ceiling. "Look, that wasn't the right way to say that—"

"Oh, so you meant to dismiss me more politely? You called me a terrible name by accident?"

"Look, I'm tired, and—"

"In pain," I finished for him as I went to the door. I paused with my hand on the doorframe and waited. He watched me with sorrow in his eyes but he made no move to stop me. I shook my head at the thought. He was in too much pain to stand. How in the world could he stop me now? "Take the fucking pills, Gabe," I said, and then I left to try and reassemble the pieces of my broken heart.

Chapter Twenty

GABE

The silence she left behind was total.

"Fuck," I whispered. I wanted to fall back into my bed, but everything hurt. Including my heart.

I'd driven her away.

I'd made a huge fucking mistake.

That night the ibuprofen couldn't even touch the throbbing. I grabbed my crutches and hopped to the bathroom. I stood by the sink and pulled the pill bottle, never opened, of opioids out of the medicine cabinet.

It fit so neatly in my hand. Like it belonged there, nestled into the crook of my palm. Just holding it seemed to give a measure of relief as every cell in my body went quiet in anticipation of the hit.

It sat heavy in my palm, too heavy, it seemed, for me to lift it. I looked down and stared at my name on the label.

It had my name on it. The pills were literally calling my name.

When the prescription came home with me I was too out of it to flush them. I'd had ample time to flush them in the weeks since, but something had stopped me.

I must have known I'd need something to help with this. Driving Everly away was a different kind of pain.

Numb, I moved to twist open the bottle. The grooves slid into place, the child-lock came loose. The cap was untwisted, ready to fall off into my other hand.

I froze in place. My heart stalled in my chest. I was so close to popping the pill, but...

I didn't take the cap off.

Slowly I exhaled. I ducked away from my reflection in the mirror, feeling like it was watching me, disappointed. Pleading. Reminding me of all those nights in rehab where I'd felt the same compulsion. The devil on my shoulder whispering encouraging words about risking it all. He'd never gone away. I'd been drowning out his voice with thoughts of Everly.

"Fuck," I whispered again. I'd been right. I didn't need her help. I needed...

Her.

Her hard-won smiles, her sass, her determination. I needed her physical presence in the room with me, her body's nearness to mine. I needed her, and I'd driven her away. Lost in my frustration at my weakness, I'd driven away the very person I needed to make me strong again.

With calm resolve, I re-latched the bottlecap and set it deliberately back into the cabinet. I shut the door on the pills.

It was only then that I realized my entire body was shaking. In fear. And in anticipation of the beautiful hit, that wonderful bliss.

"Fucking weak," I snarled in the back of my throat. Enraged, I slammed my fist into the wall, but the sting in my knuckles didn't make me feel any stronger. "I hate this shit," I muttered. All of this shit. The pain, the weakness, the helplessness. The Gabe I was before, the old me, he took these giant risks every goddamn day, put his body and his self on the line just to feel something. And here I was hiding in the bathroom after sending away the only thing that had made me *feel* in months. Fuck, I'd *found her again*, after months of wondering, and I was gonna push her away because I felt sorry for myself?

Fuck you, the old, risk-taker Gabe said to this new, wimpy Gabe. Fucking call her and tell her you're sorry.

I nodded and cleared my throat. "Fuck." I repeated it one more time because it felt necessary, but my throat was tight and dry and I couldn't get a full breath. *Don't pussy out now,* the part of me that still had pride insisted. *If you're not gonna call her then fucking text her, you weak piece of shit.*

I nodded and hopped back to my bedroom, then grabbed my phone from its place at my bedside table. Quickly, before the weakness could take hold again, I flicked to her contact and started typing.

Me: Are you up?

Lame. But it was a start.

I waited, glancing down out of my window. Her house was nestled down there by the raging creek, dark and shut up for the night. I hoped she was too pissed at me to go right to sleep.

She was.

Everly: Do you need something?

Cold. Professional. I deserved that.

Me: Yeah. I need to tell you that I'm sorry.

I waited, but she didn't reply. I glanced down at her house again. The light was still on, so I took a deep breath.

Me: I do need you. I need you around. You make everything better.

Me: And I'm sorry I haven't said that until now.

Me: Fuck, I mean I just found you.

Me: I might be an idiot, but I'm not going to let you go again.

Me: I promise.

The light went off. With my heart in my throat, I watched my screen, but there was no sign of a reply. With a heavy heart, I set my phone back down on the nightstand.

Where it glowed with a new text alert.

Everly: Open your door. I forgot my key.

Chapter Twenty-One

EVERLY

He threw open the door with such violence that it hit the wall next to it. I winced, but he didn't seem to care as he stared at me. "You came over?"

"I hate texting," I declared.

A wash of relief flooded his face and before I could say another word he had the door open and me in his arms. "I fucked up," he murmured, leaning down to cup my face in his hand, pressing tender kisses to my eyebrow, my lips, my jaw. "I'm really fucking sorry."

I sighed against his shoulder, bracing myself so he could set his crutch aside and put his arm around me.

We stood still like that for one heartbeat, ten heartbeats. As I relaxed into the sound of his breathing, a silvery light appeared at his feet. "Gabe?" I breathed, standing up and stepping back. "What's that?"

"What?"

"Your feet! They're glowing!"

He looked down in shock and then started laughing. "Babe," he said, reaching out and gently cupping my chin. "It's the moon."

He tilted my face towards the window in the door. There, hanging in the sky, was a huge, fat full moon peeking in between the racing clouds. "Oh my god," I giggled. "It's been raining for so long I forgot what the moon looked like." I buried my face in my hands.

Chuckling, he reached out and gently tugged my hands away from my face. "Come with me," he murmured. "I have something I want to tell you, but my parents' bedroom is down here and..."

"You want to sneak me into your bedroom while your parents are asleep?" I teased.

He shook his head ruefully. "I never got a chance to do that." Then he brightened as a mischievous smile spread across his face. "So yeah. I totally want to sneak a pretty girl into my bedroom for the first time tonight."

As I followed him, grinning about the scandal of it all, I wanted to keep my heart light. After all, he'd apologized in the best way possible, and my training had prepared me for how much people in pain could lash out. I was grateful for that lesson.

But my training also meant that I knew exactly how much he struggled with putting weight on his ankles. Instead of making a clinical observation, I pressed my hand to my heart in sympathy. What I saw as I watched him hobble up the stairs hurt my heart. His limp was so pronounced on his left side. When he reached the top there was no mistaking the grunt of pain as he had to pivot to reach his door.

"Gabe," I said. "You need to listen to me."

"No, I have to tell you this. Let me go first," he said as he pushed the door open.

I stepped in, pressed it closed behind me, and shook my head. "No," I said firmly. "You need to hear this."

He let out an explosive sigh, then gestured for me to continue.

"Sit," I begged. "Please." I shook my head. "As a nurse, I want you to heal. But as a person who—" I trailed off. What kind of person was I about to confess to being? A person who cared for him way too much? "I can't stand to see you struggling like this when there are ways you can help yourself."

Gabe stared at me for a long moment. When he inclined his head in a soft nod, I wondered what he had decided to tell me. My heart started racing out of some perverse defense mechanism. Even though I wanted nothing more than to stay here with him, the way he was looking at me had me ready to flee.

Finally he exhaled and patted the bed next to him. "Right," he said. "And this was what I was going to tell you, too." He glanced at me. I hadn't moved from the spot. "Please come sit by me, Everly. Standing up like that? You have to know it looks like you're showing off right now."

In spite of myself, I started laughing. When I went to him, it was with the sun shining inside of me. "What were you going to tell me?" I asked as I settled in next to him.

His thigh was pressed alongside mine. He didn't look up at me when I sat down, but he did reach over and grab my hand. He lifted my fingers, playing with each one in turn before twining them with his. "Everly, I can't take those painkillers. I can't."

I snatched my hand away. "Yes you can!" I bleated, frustration making me raise my voice. "You're only refusing to out of some kind of—"

"I can't!" he said in a low, forceful tone that stopped me mid-sentence. I stared at him and when he finally raised his eyes to mine, I felt like he'd caught me in a tractor beam. Pulling me in to him. "Everly, I've been sober two years, one month, and fourteen days."

"Sober," I echoed, not quite comprehending. Was he a drunk? Is that what he—

"Pills," he said, answering the question I hadn't dared ask. "Anything I could get my hands on, but opioids mostly. Codeine, morphine, Vicodin." He glanced away and seemed to force himself to look at me again. Shame was written in the drawn lines on his face and my chest felt too tight to catch a full breath. I reached out and snatched up his other hand, pressing it to my lips as he said, "Our manager gave me the first one, and after that, any time I needed something to take the edge off, he was right there with another little white pill for me. I mean, even if I didn't think I was on edge, he was still pushing." He growled in the back of his throat and tried to snatch his hand away in frustration, but I held on to him tightly and refused to let him pull away. He looked down at our still-joined hands as if in surprise and looked up at me with a challenge in his eyes. "I tell people it was my manager who got me hooked, but no one seems to want to believe me. They tell me to take personal responsibility and I fucking have, but it wasn't my fault."

A little alarm bell went off in my head, but I knew now was not the time to challenge him about that idea. Not while he was baring his soul to me. "Wow," I said.

He looked at me.

"You're pretty strong, you know that?"

He made a snorting sound and gestured to his legs.

I nudged him. "No, not like that. I mean... here."

Without thinking I pressed my hand to his heart. He closed his hand over it. I could feel the strong, steady *thump thump* under my fingers and there was an answering throb in my own body. My breath caught for a moment as I looked up at him again. "You've been suffering this whole time and you never told me why?"

"I haven't been suffering," he said in a voice so low I had to lean in to hear it. "Not when I'm with you."

As he said that, I felt his heart speed up under my hand and my breath quickened at his reaction. Tracing my fingers up, I instinctually started to feel for the pulse at his throat.

He caught my hands, one and then the other. "Come here," he whispered, lightly tugging.

"Are you sure? I might... I'm gonna hurt you."

"Not as much as it hurts me to have you so far away. Come here, baby. Let me hold you, please."

It was the please that propelled me forward until I was straddling his lap, facing him. I was careful not to press down with my full weight, but he grinned at my attempts to hold myself in the air and with a firm tug he yanked me flush against him. "Gabe!" I gasped, half thrilled and half worried. "Be careful!"

"I'll be careful," he promised, then he reached up and threaded his fingers into my hair, pulling me down into a kiss that made my brain melt. "I'll be so careful," he murmured against my mouth, but it was just sounds now, the shape of his words deepening the kiss as I sighed into him, the light in my chest blazing as bright as the sun at noon.

Chapter Twenty-Two

GABE

Her body against mine was strong and taut. Her mouth was hot and desperate. There were so many layers to this girl, but they were all hidden away under that shell of hers. She was always hanging back and waiting for someone else to make the first move. She was too wary to cut loose, to take a risk.

Who better to help her get over that than me?

And what better way than this? "I'll be so careful," I was saying, but it was far from a promise I could keep. Not with her straddling me like this. Not with my hands in her hair and my face in her breasts, kissing until I felt her nipples tighten into beads under my lips. "Don't hold yourself like that, Everly," I told her. "I've got you."

"I—" she started to say, then hissed through her teeth as I slid my hands back around her waist to pull her down into my lap. I knew she was feeling how much I wanted her right here, right now, but that tension was still singing through her body. "Your parents," she whispered.

I nibbled my way from the top of one rounded breast up to her neck. "Who cares?"

"Gabe, I—oh..." she moaned as I brushed my lips against her ear.

A shiver tore through her body and she arched closer to me. I grinned against her neck. "Oh, you like that, huh? What else do you like, baby? Tell me quick so I have time to do them all to you before I wear you out."

"Do that," she urged. Her eyes were half closed in pleasure as she pointed to her ear again. "Kiss me there again?"

The hesitation in her voice almost broke my heart. I wondered if this girl had ever been allowed to ask for what she wanted. What she needed.

I had a lot of work to do to show her it was okay to demand what she wanted, and I planned on enjoying every minute of it. "Right here?" I questioned, curling my tongue along her earlobe. Another delicious shudder tore through her body and it was all I could do not to groan in response. "Or do you like it better when I do this?" I nibbled along the shell of her ear before biting down.

"Unh!" Her stifled scream was music to my ears.

"You like it when I bite," I groaned in approval. "Jesus, why are you so fucking perfect?" I peppered her skin from the place under her ear right down to the pulse at her throat with little biting kisses and every time my teeth found her skin she pressed against me, swaying in this sexy little rocking rhythm that drove all of the blood in my body straight down to my cock. "Let's see if these beauties are as sensitive as your sweet little ear," I urged, coaxing her out of the flannel and oversized T-shirt she must have changed into at home.

With a glazed look in her eyes, she shrugged out of her flannel, then seemed to snap back into focus when I tugged at her shirt. "I've got it," she said.

"It's okay to accept help, you know," I couldn't help pointing out.

She stuck out her tongue at me as she lifted her shirt. I let out an appreciative hiss when I caught sight of her for the first time. She was braless under her shirt and her breasts were small and perfectly shaped, with high, proud nipples that already stood at attention as if in invitation. I glanced up at her face and caught the wary look she was giving me. "You have the prettiest tits I've ever seen."

Her face flushed and she gave me a smile that squeezed my heart. "They're small," she said, crossing her arms in front of her chest.

I gently tugged her hand away. "They're perfect and I really want to tell them how perfect they are."

She giggled. "You want to talk to my breasts?"

"I feel like they're suffering from unwarranted low self-esteem. Hey," I whispered, leaning forward and pressing my lips to her skin as I spoke. "You listen to me now. Don't ever let anyone make you think you're not fucking spectacular." When she laughed again, more freely this time, I kissed first one, then the other, and gave in to the need to cup them in my hands. "Dear God, I can't believe you've been hiding these from me all this time."

"Scrubs aren't very flattering," she sighed before squeaking as I gently took one of those pretty, pearly nipples into my mouth.

It was bliss to feel that sensitive skin tighten under my lips, but when I bit down gently and made my girl gasp in pleasure, I felt higher than any pill had ever taken me before. I bit down harder, testing how much she could take and was surprised but not really surprised that Everly wanted to skirt that edge of pain. She wanted more sensation. She wanted the feelings to shut out the noise in her head.

Just like I did.

That revelation drove all thoughts of being careful away. With a growl, I sank my teeth into the soft skin that surrounded her nipple, biting a savage ring into one breast before moving to the other. Everly moaned and squirmed in my lap, grinding her hips against me. It was far sexier than any lapdance I'd ever had, and what made it even better was that it was my name she moaned as she writhed.

Needing more, I tugged at her waistband. "Let me have all of you," I demanded, almost begging. "Stand up, baby, and let me see your pussy."

She was beyond blushing at the rough word. She hopped off my lap with an eagerness that made my cock throb painfully. When she yanked her yoga pants down past her hips, she revealed she was bare under there as well. "Naughty girl."

"I thought I was going to bed."

"You are. With me."

"Then I guess I'm dressed appropriately after all," she said, her lips twisting into a grin as she stepped out of her pants.

"Shit," I hissed. She gave me that same wary look as she watched me take her all in. I knew enough to add, "I bet you taste as good as you look."

She rocked a little on her heels, and her toes may have curled a little. "I have no idea."

"I'll let you know," I told her, reaching out and taking her hand. "I'm going to kiss your pretty pussy for a little while now. Is that okay with you?"

"Uh."

"No one's ever kissed you down there?"

She shook her head.

"Are you a virgin?"

"No," she said, her voice half frustration, half regret. "But the guy... it was just one time... and he was in a hurry... he didn't..."

I pressed my lips together and pushed down the urge to deck the knucklehead who didn't take his time with this girl. "I'm glad," I said. "Because I planned on being the standard by which you measured all guys." I grinned. "It's a good thing I have nobody you could compare me to."

"Why?"

"Because that's unfair to the other guy," I boasted as I tugged her to me. "Now, baby, I want to taste you in the worst possible way, but I need you to do something to help me."

"Of course."

I shifted and leaned back onto the bed, carefully maneuvering until I was flat on my back. She watched me and when I finally laid down she let out a breath and I knew she'd been worried I was hurting. But I wasn't feeling anything except need for her. "Ready to help me?"

"Yes, of course."

"Great." I beckoned her over. "Come sit on my face."

Chapter Twenty-Three

EVERLY

He was looking at me. And more than that, he was seeing me.

I was surprised at the eagerness with which I straddled him. My shyness fought against the overwhelming desire to be noticed and adored, and the desire won out fully when he looked up at me from between my legs.

I knelt over him, exposing my most vulnerable parts to him, and he was watching like I was some kind of sacred object. His eyes flicked to that space between my legs and then back up to my eyes as I looked down at him. "Gotta say," he murmured. "The view from down here is incredible."

Heat flowed through my veins as his fingers brushed up the inside of my thighs. "Spread your legs for me, baby. I need you down here." He touched his tongue and gave a dirty flick that made my heart skip in disbelief that this was happening to me. "Right down on my mouth, please. Yes, you're really helping me out here, thank you." He moaned almost as loud as I did when his tongue first touched my overheated skin. I leaned forward and braced my hands on the wall, looking down in utter disbelief at Gabe King's face between my legs. For a moment I could only assume this was some kind of fever dream brought on from stress.

But then his tongue started moving and that worry fled my brain. Along with any thoughts about professionalism, the fact that his parents were downstairs, the fact that I wasn't acting like myself at all. Was I really the kind of girl who could strip naked and straddle a former rockstar's face? Was I really a girl who a former rockstar would even notice?

Up until an hour ago I would have answered no to both of those questions and yet here I was, naked and grinding myself against Gabe King's tongue as he made appreciative and encouraging noises. The hum of his lips against my clit went straight to my core, making my thighs tense and quake. I braced my hands against the wall, scraping my nails against the plaster as he swirled his tongue around the entrance of my pussy before lapping it in a series of small, perfect thrusts. My whole body was taut and ready, poised at the edge so that when he slid his tongue back up to my clit and flattened it so that the whole of my sex was covered in the warm pressure, it was like a bomb went off under my skin.

"Gabe, shit, Gabe..." My powers of speech dissolved completely, leaving me with nothing but mindless babble to express what I was thinking. Fuck, I wasn't thinking, I was only feeling the explosion roil outward to my limbs. "Gabe, fuck, Gabe..." Even as the orgasm pulsed through me, I was already greedy for more. More than his tongue could give. I wanted to hear his moans unmuffled. I wanted to watch his face as he sank inside of me and see if he watched with that same rapt attention.

I wanted to fuck Gabe King more than I'd ever wanted anything in my life.

"Fuck," he groaned, still swirling that greedy tongue around. "You do taste as good as you look. I can fucking feel you coming on my tongue. You're phenomenal, baby, you're fucking spectacular." He reached up, bracing my still-quivering thighs, and pressed me down to sit on his chest as the aftershocks of the orgasm he'd just given me ricocheted through my body. "I want to eat you all night long, baby, so take a break."

"No," I moaned.

"No?"

I reached down, trailing my fingers down his chest and stomach. I could feel his muscles quivering with the strain of pent-up desire and when my fingers closed around his length, he let out a moan that sounded more like an explosion. "No," I said as I began to move my hand in time with his arching hips. "I want to fuck you, Gabe."

"Christ, you really are phenomenal," he said as he watched me stroke the outside of his jeans with a reverent gaze.

I wasn't experienced at all. My one sexual experience could hardly be counted as experience since it was accomplished in the teacher's bathroom of Crown Creek High. I never knew if Hal Finley actually liked me or if he was looking for an easy way to get his rocks off, but I had been thrilled enough by his attention that I readily agreed to follow him into the restroom and take off my pants. It had been quick and painful and when it was over, he'd barely looked at me.

He never looked at me again.

But Gabe was looking at me, and that knowledge made me bold. With trembling fingers, I unzipped his jeans and helped him shimmy out of them, taking care not to knock his swollen ankles. I paused before I pulled down his boxers and he lifted his head to catch my eye. "You okay?" he asked in a voice suffused with such care and longing that it undid me.

"I'm good," I said, and I meant it more than he could ever know.

When I pulled his boxers down, I had to stop and remind myself that this was not the first time I was seeing his cock. It was just the first time I was seeing it hard and perfect like that. Standing at a ninety-degree angle from his body, it looked so silken and smooth that I was taken with a desire to lick it. I leaned down and kissed the head, surprised at how it felt against my lips. Gabe breathed out a ragged, "Ah!" which only made me want to make him make that sound again. I opened my mouth and closed my lips around him, and he let another "Ah!" escape. Without meaning to I made the same noise in my throat.

I'd always thought of giving a guy head as something passive and subservient, but kneeling over Gabe and drawing those guttural moans from him every time I slid my lips down his shaft was the most powerful I had ever felt. I got greedy, moving faster, little slurping sounds escaping my mouth in my haste to take all of him in.

I felt his big hands on my head. "Baby, you keep doing that, I'm gonna come in your mouth, and I don't want to be done just yet," he groaned, closing my hair in his fists.

I sat up and he swore. "Fuck, look at you with those swollen lips. Come here and kiss me."

I crawled up to him and he sealed his mouth to mine in the most bruising kiss of my life. When I blinked back, breathless and gasping, his eyes were darker than I'd ever seen them. "There's a condom in my nightstand right there," he rumbled.

My fingers trembled in excitement, making the process of extracting the foil packet from the package feel like it took eons. "Can you?" I asked him shyly. "I've never..."

With a warm smile, he deftly plucked the wrapper from my hand and I watched, fascinated, as he gripped himself and quickly unrolled the condom onto his cock. "You're gonna ride me, right, baby? Because I'm getting really addicted to looking up at those tits."

I bit my lip. *This* was an addiction I could definitely support. With his eyes on me, I felt like the most beautiful thing in the world as I straddled him once again and guided his cock inside of me. "Slowly, baby," he murmured as I hissed at that first burning stretch. "I'm not in any rush. You make it good for you."

I nodded and slid myself down in tiny increments, feeling the way he filled and stretched me. He hissed again as I began to move, taking him in with short shallow strokes. "Oh my god," I breathed as I looked down to where his cock was sliding inside of me.

"Look at us, baby. We fit so good together," he said, reaching out and cupping his hands around my ass cheeks, guiding me deeper. When he sank in all the way to the hilt, we both gasped. I could feel him throbbing inside of me, growing even harder.

"Shit," I whispered, leaning forward. His pubic bone ground into my clit as I started to ride him, gasping. He growled and put his hand on my back, pressing me down so that all the movement was concentrated right in that spot as he somehow thrust upward. I was on top of him, but he was in control, taking me closer and closer to the edge every time we came together.

"Yes, like that, Jesus, get there, Everly, because you feel too fucking good. Right like that, I can feel you. You're so tight, fuck, I want you to come on my cock, you hear me?" There was no teasing in his voice now. He was all authority and animal desire. "I'm gonna fuck you like this until you come for me."

That exquisite friction was driving me out of my mind. I planted my hands on his chest, and I could feel his heart racing under my fingers in a pace that matched my own. "Gabe!" I cried, half begging, half triumphant, and the wave of pressure that had been building broke across me.

I exploded. I fucking lost my mind.

"Gabe!"

I rode him like a wild woman, chasing that incredible sensation as it went on and on, shocking me with its intensity even as I wanted it to go on forever. When I thought it was starting to ebb, I felt his cock twitch inside of me and Gabe roared, sinking his fingers into my hips and pulling me down so hard our bodies slapped together, skin on skin, the drum solo in the concert we were putting on for each other.

Chapter Twenty-Four

GABE

I pushed myself up to catch her as she fell against me. Our breathing slowed and synced up. Holding her like this, feeling the sweat on her skin and smelling our mingled scents, was important enough to me that I was able to ignore the sharp pain in my ribs from supporting myself like this.

I kissed her shoulder. Running my hand up the curve of her spine, it was a wonder to me that I had ever not known her. Once I had her in my arms it was as clear as muscle memory that she was the girl I'd been dreaming about all this time. "Baby," I breathed.

She knew at once what I was about to say. "Lie down," she ordered.

I grinned. "Yes, nurse."

She nodded and slid off the bed and yanked on her clothes. "Be right back."

"I'm not going anywhere," I reminded her.

She disappeared from the room and returned with a wet cloth. "Hygiene is an important part of the healing process," she intoned with a cute little smirk on her face.

I rolled my eyes. "It's a good thing you're my nurse, because I wouldn't let anyone else in the world do this."

Her eyes widened as she watched me clean myself. "It is a good thing I'm your nurse," she agreed, moving to kiss me. Then she stopped with a stricken look on her face. "Oh my god." She buried her face in her hands.

I shook my head and gently tugged them away. "None of that." I leaned up, searching her face. "You're freaking out. Why are you freaking out?"

"I'm going to lose this job," she said.

I wanted to laugh and tell her it didn't matter, but I knew how much it mattered to her. How much she needed the money. I stifled my laugh and was about to protest that I'd make sure she was taken care of when something flickered across her face. Her chin jutted stubbornly. "Right. I'm done with it."

"What?"

"This job. I slept with my patient. That's completely unprofessional. I'm definitely fired." She looked almost relieved.

"Does that mean you're not coming over anymore?" I slid my hands between her legs.

She arched into it. "Don't know why I would," she said, but there was something I loved about the way her lip twitched in glee.

"Hmm, you don't know why?" I flicked my tongue out. "Maybe I can persuade you to stop by once in a while?"

"Not as your nurse," she said firmly. "I officially quit."

I grinned. I knew how important this was to her, that she stay professional on the job. So of course it would make sense that she wouldn't want the job any more. "Yup, you don't even have to give your two-weeks notice. But maybe you could come over as my girl?"

Her face lit up like she had the sun shining from inside of her. "As your girl?" Her grin grew crafty. "Yeah. I suppose I could do that." She leaned over and kissed me. "I should go now, though," she whispered.

It broke my heart that she couldn't stay. I wanted to lie next to her and listen to her breathing deepen as she fell asleep and press the curve of her body against mine. "This fucking hospital bed," I growled. "It's too tiny."

She pulled her shirt over her head and leaned over to kiss my nose. "But I told you I was coming back."

I nodded firmly. "As my girl."

"As your girl." She kissed my lips.

"Good night, Everly."

"Sleep well, Gabe."

"I will. You wore me right out."

She blushed and ducked her head as she scurried out the door, but I took a perverse sense of pride in seeing she was walking a little bowlegged.

I was still feeling blissed out and sated when I mindlessly reached out to my phone to check what time it was.

"Fuck," I whispered when I saw the missed call notification. I recognized the area code. I knew who it had to be, but part of me didn't dare hope.

I pressed the play button and my producer's voice boomed out of the speaker. "Gabriel! Listen, sorry to be calling so late. I know you're probably asleep or something, but I wanted to get ahold of you with the good news as soon as I got it. We're renewed!" I heard him slap his palm on his thigh and could picture him sitting there in the corner office late at night, his feet up on his huge oaken desk.

Kit Lomber was the producer of King of Pain. Me taking giant risks on camera had pretty much paid for that ritzy corner office. "Call me as soon as you get this and we can talk scheduling," he went on. "I know we need to work around your recovery and all, but I know you're gonna be back on your feet and jumping off buildings again real soon, buddy." He paused like he was about to hang up, then repeated his plea with a note of desperation in his voice. "Call me."

I looked at the screen, my finger already hovering over the call back button. Getting back to the show had been all I wanted these past few frustrating months. Getting paid to do stupid, thrilling shit? Hell, I'd fucking do it for free. I couldn't wait to get back.

Except.

I glanced at the door. Everly's scent still hung in the room, clinging to my skin and filling my lungs. She'd said she'd come over as my girl, but would she still want to be my girl if I told her I was leaving? Was I leaving?

If you'd asked me last week if I planned on staying in Crown Creek once I healed, I would have laughed at you. But now?

Now I wasn't laughing at all.

Chapter Twenty-Five

EVERLY

It was one of those days where everything lines up.

I woke before my alarm with a ton of energy. I weighed myself and noted with glee that I had lost two pounds—probably from the workout Gabe gave me last night, I remembered with a pleasing warmth in my belly. I brewed my coffee perfectly and the newly restored Grim started right up, as obedient as a well-trained dog. I hit all the lights on my way in to class and I didn't even mind that all of my classmates were still discussing when the boards results would be posted. I was going to take them the next time they were given. No big deal.

Who was this new girl that everything came easily to?

Me, I thought giddily as I snagged a parking spot right next to the door.

I was so used to everything going wrong that I'd padded a lot of time into my morning out of habit. Since everything had gone right, I was the first one to arrive for class, a full half hour before it was supposed to start.

I stepped in and let the door close behind me, but a gust of wind from someone entering down the hall caught it and sent it slamming shut with a bang that made me jump.

A muffled cry came from behind the podium. Startled, I looked down the rows to see a face poking out, crumpled with a yawn. Her tight French braid was fuzzy and falling down with sleep.

"Rachel?" I called.

She leaped to her feet. "Please don't tell," she said, yanking at her rumpled clothes and re-tucking her shirt in.

I stared at her, horrified. "Is this where you sleep?" I asked her.

She pressed her lips together, and I cursed myself for even asking. "Is class starting?" she asked, and I realized it was more words than she'd said to me thus far.

I shook my head. "No, I'm early."

She looked relieved and stifled another yawn.

I felt my heart tweak in sympathy. I didn't know the girl, but I had the distinct feeling that she and I had a lot in common. We both moved around the edges of things, wary and waiting for someone to notice us.

Gabe had noticed me. I'd noticed her.

This was the morning where everything was going right. That was the only reason I had the courage to suggest what I said next. "In fact," I said, setting down my books. "I was just heading over to the student union to grab some coffee." I hadn't planned on this at all, but she didn't need to know that. "You want to come?" I asked hesitantly. "You look like you could use some help waking up."

She looked at me warily. She had soft brown eyes that held some kind of childish innocence. Even braided, her dark blonde hair fell to the small of her back. She seemed far too young and naive to be an adult in the working world, yet that's exactly what she was. "I have to start working in half an hour," she said in a warning tone that sounded like it was a reminder to herself.

I grinned. "That's more than enough time."

A flickering fear danced across her face, but she quickly composed herself. Nodding, she followed me as we hurried through the lashing rain across the concrete plaza to the student union building. "Their coffee isn't the best here," I yelled over the wind, needing to fill the silence somehow. "But it's hot and warms my hands up, and at least makes me feel like I *should* be awake. Maybe it's a psychosomatic response, you know?"

I glanced at Rachel, who smiled but only slightly. She followed behind me through the ordering line. "What would you like?" I asked her.

"The same as you," she demurred.

I paid for both of them, then handed hers over. "Thank you," she said, holding it away from her body like she was afraid of it."

I set mine down at one of the wobbly tables and took off the lid. "Do you take milk and sugar?" I asked.

Her face fell. All at once she sat down in the chair like someone had swiped her legs out from under her.

My nursing instincts kicked into high gear. "Are you faint?" I demanded. "Have you eaten?"

She looked up at me. "I'm okay," she said. I widened my eyes when I heard how different her voice sounded. Gone was the breathy deference, and in its place was a kind of steely confidence that made me wonder what this girl had gone through—and wonder about those she'd left in her wake. "I was just realizing that I have no idea how I like my coffee."

The way she said it, it sounded like a huge confession, but I couldn't figure out why it was a revelation. "I think it's better with a little bit of cream and one teaspoon of sugar," I said.

She nodded. "Okay."

Confused, I went over to the creamers, carefully prepared hers exactly the way I prepared mine, and brought it back. "Here you go," I said.

She took a deep breath before taking a sip, then she licked her lips. She looked up at me. "This is the first time I've ever tasted coffee," she said in that new, confident voice.

I blinked. "First time?"

She set the cup down and closed her eyes, then opened them like she was making a decision to trust me. "My religion forbade it," she said.

"Your religion? Are you Mormon?"

She shook her head and looked down.

The realization hit me in slow-motion waves, lapping at the shore again and again until I was able to say it. "You're one of God's Chosen?" I asked. I'd never seen them working out in the community before. I've never seen their women wearing pants before, either. I'd also never been spoken to by any of them as they moved like shadows through our community, ghosts we all saw but never spoke of.

Rachel wasn't a ghost, that much was clear.

She lifted her gaze to me and her eyes were direct and clear and more than a little fierce. "Not anymore," she said firmly.

Chapter Twenty-Six

GABE

I stomped around the quiet house, boredom nipping at my heels. Everly had class all day and then clinical hours at the hospital, and the knowledge that it would be at least twenty-four hours until I could be with her again had me pacing like a jungle cat at the zoo.

I was mostly healed now. As long as I moved carefully and took frequent breaks, I was able to move normally again.

Normally for regular people, anyway. For me it was almost worse than before, to have command of my body again but not be able to do what I wanted with it.

My family could see that the cabin fever was getting to me. Yesterday, my mother had come home with an armful of thick, heavy books, plonking them down on my bedside table with a wordless smile. She'd brought me a bunch of true-adventure stuff, memoirs of risk-takers doing incredible things.

She meant well, and I tried to appreciate it. But I'd read exactly ten pages of one of them before I needed to stand. Sitting there reading about other people's lives being lived to the fullest while I sat there in the quiet bedroom made my skin itchy.

I stalked around in the house, my mind a perfect blank, until I ended up in Beau's room.

If you'd asked me right then what my plan was, I would have sworn that I had none. I hadn't come in here with any purpose in mind.

Then I saw it.

My tablet.

I knew why I was there.

He hadn't even attempted to hide it. Probably thought I was well enough to be trusted, now. A promise was a promise, so I wasn't about to start watching the video of my fall again.

I grabbed it and sat down, stretching my legs way out. I hesitated, then tapped a few keys, calling up YouTube. Then I tapped a few more keys and settled back. There it was—that same illicit thrill I felt when I watched my fall. In a way, this was the same as watching my old self die.

A few chiming notes sounded, and then an overblown "ah ah ah" choral that made me grimace. Hands fluttered across the screen, then turned into a dove.

Then—

Noelle.

I inhaled sharply when my ex's face filled the screen. I stared as she sang, that sweet voice that used to raise goosebumps on my skin.

She had torn out my soul as well as my heart, but there was still that ache in my chest that she'd left behind. As I watched, I slowly realized that ache was a part of my old self that had belonged only to her.

I wasn't that guy anymore. That old self had died, and I was here now. I watched her, waiting for the feelings to resurrect themselves, like ghosts in my cells. But the more I watched, the more I felt...

Nothing.

She was just another pretty blonde girl. Bubbly and sweet-voiced, nothing more and nothing less. I didn't feel angry anymore, only a strange kind of nostalgia. She was a part of my life that had passed. It was over, and I'd moved on to something better.

I pressed stop, freezing Noelle in place. I lifted the tablet and stared into those wide blue eyes. "I'm done," I told her.

Then I closed the browser and carefully set the tablet back onto my brother's desk.

When I walked away, I didn't even limp.

I got exactly as far as Beau's doorway, only to come face to face with my younger brother as he came up the stairs.

He'd caught me red-handed snooping in his room. If it had been Finn, I'd be getting a beat-down even now. But since this was Beau, he gave me one of his level looks. "You need something?"

I let out a long breath. "Yeah. A dirt bike and a hundred-foot jump."

He grinned. "Yeah...you're not gonna find that in my room, though," he pointed out. Then he widened his eyes a little. "But what you will find is this."

He shoved past me and went right over to his guitar stand. "Here," he said.

I swallowed and stared at the instrument. My brother held it out to me in some mix of encouragement and accusation.

I hadn't played since the band broke up. Without my brothers around me, the idea of making music didn't seem the same.

I took it from him anyway. Call it reflex. Call it curiosity. I slung the strap around my neck with careless confidence. I moved my fingers to the strings.

Then I stopped. "I don't think I remember how," I said slowly. I pressed down on the frets and winced. "My callouses are all gone."

My brother gave me an encouraging nod. "You'll pick it up again. It's like riding a bike."

I tested out a few hesitant chords. "Are you still playing?" I asked him. I hadn't heard any strumming come from his room.

He shook his head. "Guitar was never really my thing."

I nodded. Beau was a competent enough guitar player, but he only did it when he had to. "Are you playing your big-ass piano still?" I asked.

Beau's eyes got a little foggy looking. "Not here as much. I found an even nicer one at the high school. It's got the kind of tone I always wanted, but those little keyboards were so synthetic. Big and round and full."

"You know you look like a total weirdo when you play," I reminded him.

"I have passion," he said primly.

Why did that make me feel defensive? "I have plenty of passion."

"Your passion is getting your shit fucked up," Beau said, his mild tone taking the sting out of his words. "We always knew you didn't have music in you."

Now I was really feeling attacked "I have music in me," I protested.

"It's okay, man. You are a good technical player. You have a good enough ear to fake it." Beau lifted his chin a little and grinned. "It was enough for our purposes, right?"

The way he smiled, I could tell he meant nothing by it, but it still stung. "Fuck you, then," I grumbled, clutching the guitar close and stalking back to my room.

I spent the rest of the night starting from scratch. I got out all my old instruction books, and even played along with a few of our old songs, humming my harmonies along with my brothers' recorded voices. I was up so late that sleep overtook me. I woke up right next to the guitar and started practicing again.

It was only after I'd retuned it and picked my way through all the major and minor scales that I realized Beau had outwitted me. He knew I'd rather play music again than admit he was right.

Chapter Twenty-Seven

EVERLY

"Coffee is magic," Rachel grinned.

We'd been meeting before my Monday, Wednesday, and Friday classes for three weeks now, and in that span of time she'd developed a wicked caffeine addiction. "I can see why they forbade us drinking it," she went on, cupping it in both hands before taking another sip. "I feel like I could take down a house. Or run a marathon."

Her pupils were dilated the size of dinner plates. "Okay, champ," I said, reaching over and gently prying the cup from her hands. "Let's go easy on it, okay? You've got years of addiction to make up for before you can keep up with me."

She laughed. We sat in the Student Union on a drizzly April afternoon. On the wall next to our table was the message board where clubs and groups posted their flyers. "They need to take down that one for the Blood Drive," I commented as I glanced over it. "That already happened."

"So take it down," Rachel said.

I gave her a look. "If I get up from this table are you going to suck down the rest of this coffee in one gulp?"

"Yes I am," she said with such prim dignity that I had to give in.

"Fine," I said, sliding my chair back. "That flyer's been driving me nuts."

I went over and yanked it down, exposing the post that had been hidden underneath. A house for rent—a small, two-bedroom cabin on Ridge Point Road. I knew that area. It used to be blocks of summer cabins situated on a low spit of land formed where the creek divided south of town, forking into two branches before coming together again a half mile downstream.

Without really knowing what I was doing, I yanked that flyer down too. Rachel watched me as I thoughtfully tucked it into my bag, but she didn't ask me about it. She was good at keeping her thoughts to herself. I appreciated that about her. It was something that friends did.

I had a friend.

I sat back down and took the coffee cup from her hands with a shake of my head. My friend smiled with that little twist of her head, looking down as she did. It was this little tic she had, like she was afraid to let you see her smile. "What are you doing after class?" she asked.

I blinked. "I honestly have no idea," I sighed. "I've been working my ass off, running this insane schedule for so long that now that I have a moment to myself I don't know how to relax."

"I get that feeling," she agreed. "The rest of the janitors all complain about being exhausted, but I used to clean the whole house and care for all my little sisters and brothers." That small twist of her head again. I could tell it hurt to mention them. "And after that, I'd still have to work with the rest of the women to get the meals done. Only having to look out for myself is so easy, I'm kind of bored."

I grinned at her. "Well, as your official ambassador into the world of secular hedonism, I can't have you bored. I was going to go visit Gabe—"

"Is that what you secular hedonists call it? Visiting?"

I did a double take. "Oh, oh! You're catching on fast!" I laughed. Something in my chest unclenched, the tight fist that had held my breath in its grasp loosening. Rachel was smiling too, a smug little grin as she reached over and swiped the coffee cup back from me. "I feel like I'm corrupting a little baby lamb."

She shook her head. "My older sister told me things. And you learn a lot growing up on a farm," she said.

"Come on over with me," I said. "If you really want to be like a normal girl, then you need to know who the King Brothers are."

"They're a musical group, right?"

"They were the obsession of every girl our age the whole time we were growing up," I corrected.

"Including you?"

I felt the hair on my scalp raise a little. "I had a crush on one of them, yeah."

"Gabe?"

"Jonah."

Rachel clapped her hands together in glee. "Oh my gracious, does Gabe know?"

"No!" I said, clapping my hand over her mouth. "And you can't tell him, either. He absolutely hates being overshadowed by his brother. It would drive him nuts."

"I solemnly swear to never breathe a word," Rachel said.

I glowered at her. "I feel like I should get you a Bible to swear on or something."

She shook her head. "It would have to be the Prophet's Missives," she said, and the way she said it told me that those two words were capitalized in her brain. "The Bible is corrupted by Man's touch."

"Wow," I whistled. "Don't let my mom hear you say that."

Rachel looked stricken for a moment, then let out a sigh of laughter. "Oh my word, I love caffeine!" she crowed, gulping down the last dregs from her cup.

I grinned at her. "Wait 'til you try alcohol."

Her eyes widened, scandalized. "Devil's water."

"Oh, yeah." I nodded eagerly. "You think you feel good now? Just you wait."

Rachel looked eager, so I did some quick calculations. I couldn't very well ask Gabe to come out to the bar with us, so it would have to be later in the night. Meaning I wouldn't be home for 9:30 curfew. I'd been sneaking out so often to run over to Gabe's, but going to the bar would require me taking the car. There was no way I'd be able to pull in again without waking my parents.

I pressed my lips together. "Hang on. I need to send my mother a text and tell her I'll be out. She's not going to like it, so I'm going to have to stay out until after she leaves. That's not until two, which is when the bar closes anyway. You think you'll be able to hang with me until then?"

"Gee," Rachel said. "You have to account for your whereabouts more than I ever did."

I looked up from my phone and stared at her. She smiled in her sweet way. "I guess I'm not the only one who grew up with controlling parents."

"No, I mean, it's not like that..." I started to say, but she raised her eyebrow in a way that silenced me.

Rachel had grown up under an oppressive, autocratic authority figure who made her feel shame every time she dared deviate from their rigid expectations.

Hadn't I done the same thing?

"You're right," I said, completely awestruck. I reached down and brushed my hand over the flyer I had taken from the bulletin board without truly understanding why. "Hey," I asked her. "You want to take a drive with me real quick?"

We pulled on to Ridge Point Road exactly eight minutes later, and I noted with satisfaction how close it was to school. The low-slung gray house hugged the banks of the creek like a lover. I got out of the car and pulled my hood up against the rain and grinned at Rachel, who looked shyly hopeful for me. "Look at that! If it ever stops raining, I could open the window at night and hear the creek," I said, already relishing the idea of deep quiet. "It'd be like having a white nose machine."

Rachel gave me that smile—the one that said she had no idea what I was talking about but didn't want me to spend the time to explain it.

I stared at the little place, already dreaming of being on my own. I glanced down at the flyer again as cold reality smacked me in the face. "But I can't afford the rent," I sighed. "I'd need a housemate."

Rachel was quiet. I looked over at her. Her eyes were cast downward.

That's why she had looked so hopeful. "Rachel? Where are you living these days?"

"Hi-Lo Hotel," she said softly. I hated when the confidence dripped out of her voice like that. "Everything for rent requires a security deposit and I haven't been able to—"

"Rachel?" I asked my first real friend. "Would you like to live here with me?"

Chapter Twenty-Eight

GABE

When Everly called to tell me she was moving out of her parents' house, I jumped up and down for the very first time since my accident.

Then I came over to help her start packing.

She met me at the back door with a grin and a finger to her lips. "My parents are sleeping," she whispered.

I furrowed my eyebrows. "It's the middle of the day."

"I know," she hissed. "That's why I need to move out."

I stepped in and closed the door quietly behind me, then kissed her hello. "How'd they take the news?" I asked.

She lifted her mouth into a wry smile. "I think my mother wanted to ground me, then realized that wouldn't exactly work. Then the two of them called my sister to try to get her on their side."

"How did that go?" I wondered. Everly's sister was still a mystery to me.

Her smile widened. "Abby cheered for me and then told them living in this house was like being a plant with no sunlight. They started fighting and I went upstairs and got a bunch of packing done in the meantime."

I kissed her. "You're spectacular."

"You keep saying that."

"Stop being so spectacular and I'll stop."

She grinned and gestured for me to head up to her room. This was the first time I'd ever been in the Fosters' house, even after all these years of being neighbors. It was big enough, but there was an air of closeness that hung in each room, like the walls were pressing me down with invisible hands on my shoulders. I had the strangest urge to sit.

Instead, I bounded up the stairs.

"Stop," Everly ordered when we got to the top.

I knew what she was going to say, so I took another five steps and added a little hop at the end as I turned to see my girl staring at me, open-mouthed. "You're walking so well!"

"I know."

"Doesn't it hurt still?"

"Nah, baby. I'm on this new prescription that has me feeling better than I have in a long time."

Her suspicious eyebrows first zoomed upward and then back down again as her eyes narrowed. "You have a new prescription?"

"You wrote it for me," I told her, pulling her to me and inhaling the scent of her shampoo. "Take two of these and call me in the morning."

She squealed as I cupped each of her breasts in turn and then swatted me away as she glanced out the door of her bedroom. "I can't believe you'd do that with my parents in the next room."

"We do things with *my* parents in the next room," I pointed out.

She rolled her eyes but couldn't hide the delighted smirk on her face. "Well, I don't care how good your new prescription has you feeling. Sit down. Your nurse's orders."

I sighed and sat down at the edge of her tiny bed. "And how, exactly, am I supposed to be helping you move out if you won't let me pack anything?"

"I told you I didn't need help. You came over anyway. It's not like I'm taking a whole lot with me."

"You need help carrying boxes." I glanced down at my phone. "That's why Beau should be here in a few minutes."

"Beau's coming? Why?"

I shifted on the bed, trying to find a way to sit comfortably on the tiny mattress. From the looks of things, she hadn't gotten a new bed since she was in kindergarten. "Well," I said. "I told him you needed help and he said he'd come by."

She colored and blinked back to her tiny, child-sized bookshelf. The blue of her eyes got intensely turquoise. "Baby?" I asked her, alarmed. "What's wrong?"

She abruptly shook her head and dashed her hands hastily against her cheeks. Then she smiled. "Nothing," she said brightly. "Just, you know. Moving out."

"It's gotta be weird," I agreed. "Hell, I'm still in my childhood bedroom, too."

She gave me an exasperated look. "Yeah, but you've lived other places. Me, I'm like—" She trailed off again, a faraway look in her eyes.

I thought I recognized it. It was far from standing at the edge of a bridge waiting for your turn to bungee jump, but it was the same idea. It's fucking hard to force yourself to make that leap into the unknown. "Come over here," I told her, patting the bed.

She set down the box and came over, a pile of books still clutched in her hand. "I'm proud of you, you know," I told her.

"Really? Why?"

"Because you're taking the first steps."

"You should see the house. It's a total dump."

"You'll make it a home, I'm positive." I grinned. "And you'll have me around to mess it back up again."

She gave me a shy smile. "You're gonna come over a lot?"

"Baby, you're gonna need to keep a bat by the door to shoo me away," I promised, pulling her in to me.

Even as I did, I felt my heart sink. I was promising something that could never happen. As soon as I was fully healed, my producer wanted me on a plane, ready to shoot the second season of King of Pain. The viral video of my near-death experience had made the buzz around the new season almost deafening, and Kit was rabid to start filming the second I left Crown Creek.

I brushed my hand up to cup it around Everly's arm and gave it a guilty squeeze. Her suggestive smile made it pretty clear that she had no idea the thoughts that were going through my head, but I was pretty sure I could tell the ones that were running through hers. "When is Beau supposed to get here?"

I laughed, shaking free the cobwebs of guilt. We still had time. And right now, this girl was amazing. "You little devil, you," I whispered, glancing in the direction of her parents' room.

She wiggled in my arms, doing this cute little shimmy. "Can I tell you something? You're the first boy I've ever had in my room."

A hot rush of desire made my cock press painfully against my jeans. I shifted, ready to pull her to me, and as I did the books went tumbling from her arms. Instinct made me jerk back—gotta protect those ribs—and as I did, I caught sight of a familiar face.

"Is that—" I reached for the notebook that was half hidden under the book pile.

"Give me that!" she said, trying to snatch it from my hand. But I was too quick. Loopy, girlish handwriting covered the front, and there—grinning up at me with his cheesy smile—was my brother's face.

"Mrs. Jonah King?" I read, turning the notebook this way and that. "Is that what that says?"

"Shut up," she hissed, her face beet red.

I glanced up at her with my eyes wide and opened it, leafing through the carefully cut-and-pasted pages. My brother standing. My brother sitting. My brother there in the front during a photoshoot I remembered as being particularly annoying. I flicked through the pages with an increasing sense of befuddlement. "What is this?"

She opened her mouth, then closed it, her cheeks flushing an even deeper red. "I was...a fan."

"Of...Jonah?" I leafed through page by page. "Is that...?"

She reached out and covered the picture with her hand. "Gabe!" she warned.

"You're in a *wedding dress.*" I looked down at the partially obscured collage and nudged her fingers to the side. "This is actually pretty nicely done. I bet if you ran it through Photoshop, it would really look like you were marrying my brother."

"Gabe, stop."

As much as I wanted to, I was on a roll. The old jealousy of my brother and his status as our bandleader swelled up inside of me, demanding to know if my girl still liked him better than she liked me. It was wrong and irrational, and I knew it, but I couldn't stop myself from needling her. "Did you cut his picture out of People magazine?" I glanced up at her. "You did know we lived next door to you, right? You could have asked for a picture. Or, hell, you could have just taken one from the other side of the creek."

"Gabe." She looked like she didn't know whether to cry or murder me.

I licked my lips. Getting upset was stupid. But still. "This is freaking hilarious. I'm sorry."

She relaxed a little. "You're not pissed?"

"I mean...you had shitty taste in King Brothers," I said, more stung than I wanted to admit. "But it's just weird to see, considering we're—"

"There's nothing weird about a teenaged girl having a crush," she interrupted, snatching the notebook away.

As she did, a piece of white paper slid free from where it had been tucked into the pages. I turned it over and laughed way too loudly. "You made wedding invitations, too?"

"Gabe!" she hissed and snatched it away. I was pettily gratified that she crumpled it into a ball and tossed it into her waste paper basket.

"You did a really nice job with the lettering, by the way."

"Stop."

"I love all the curlicues. Nice touch."

She clapped her hands over her face. "I was a kid."

"I remember now," I mused. "The way you used to peek over at him."

She looked up at me, stricken. "You're mad."

"I'm really not, I swear. It's just...weird," I repeated.

"I had a crush on him. *Had*," she said, the corner of her mouth turning up. She set the notebook down and brushed her hand down the side of my face. "I like to think that these days I have better taste in King Brothers."

I licked my lips, all my hurt pride melting away as she stroked her thumb over my lips. "Speaking of taste," I said, nipping at her thumb. "I have this strange urge to find out if you taste any different in this bed compared to mine." I pulled her to me and nipped at her lip, giving her that slight edge of pain I knew she liked with her pleasure. She responded by climbing onto my lap and pulling my face to hers.

I loved the way she wavered between hesitation and going for it. It was the same as asking Rachel to be her housemate and finding a little house where they could live all within the same week. She bided her time, watchful and waiting, and then, when she was sure of something, she made her move.

And I loved how sure she was of me.

I let her cup my face and kiss me until I could feel her hips start rocking against my lap. Then I pulled out my magic trick and lifted her in my arms.

I still wasn't sure enough on my feet to stand completely, but I was strong enough now to be able to lower her onto her bed. Her eyes were wide, and I grinned. "I've been doing my exercises religiously."

"I hope you're not overdoing it," she chided.

"Only where you're concerned." She grinned as I leaned over her and kissed her, slipping my hand down her body and under the waistband of her pants. She groaned in my mouth and I hissed in return to find that she was already wet for me. I drew my fingers out and touched them to my tongue as she stared. "I *think* you taste as sweet as ever, but I can't be sure unless my tongue is down there, too."

"My parents," she murmured, but she didn't stop me as I tugged her jeans down her hips.

"Lift that pretty ass for me," I urged. "Dammit, Everly, I swear that someday I'm gonna fuck you in a normal-sized bed," I complained as I shifted down and perched myself at the narrow edge of this tiny bed. "A fucking California King where we can move around and..."

She sat up and silenced me with a kiss. Searing and hot, her tongue slid against mine until I'd forgotten everything except the feel of her. I groaned and sank my hands into her hair, loving the way it twined into my fist, making it easier to hold her and kiss her properly. She whimpered as I nipped at her plump bottom lip and I used that moment to slide my fingers between her legs again. She moaned into my mouth when my thumb circled her clit, then screamed in her throat when my forefinger dipped inside of her.

I held her fast in that kiss, tugging gently at her hair until she was a mindless mass of sensations. I felt her pussy tighten around my fingers as I stroked that special place inside of her, timing my finger thrusts with strokes of my thumb over her clit. She clung to me, shuddering around my fingers as I swallowed her moans and gasps and pleas, until her whole body went rigid.

I groaned as her pussy muscles clamped down on my finger like a vise and my cock throbbed in jealousy of my fingers as she started to fall to pieces around me. I thrust my tongue into her mouth and devoured her sounds as she came over and over again until I felt her body go limp.

"Fuck, baby," I breathed. "That was intense."

"Condom," she moaned.

"In my wallet."

"Hurry," she breathed. "I need you."

I'd never moved so fast in my life. Injuries be damned, I was naked and rolling the condom on in three seconds flat. She moved to straddle me again, but I pressed my hand to her chest. "No, baby," I told her. "Today I'm gonna fuck you. Lie back and spread those legs for me."

Her eyes went dark and heavy-lidded. She reclined back on her bed like a princess and I positioned myself over her. "Wider, baby. Give me those hips."

She arched up and I plunged into her in one smooth motion.

I saw stars. I saw the fucking fabric of the universe. That searing heat burned me from the inside out and I was close to coming before I was ready. Desperate, I deliberately leaned over her in a way that put pressure on my ankle. The pain brought me back from the brink long enough that I was able to focus again and finally fuck her the way I'd been wanting to all this time.

"Gabe." Fuck, I loved the way she said my name while I was inside of her. And I definitely loved the little yelps of pleasure that escaped her lips every time I thrust into her. I was being way too rough, pounding into her with an unexplained urgency, but she took everything I had and kept asking for more, no, *pleading* for it with her eyes, her lips, and the arch of her back as she lifted herself up off the bed to brush her spectacular tits against my chest.

She needed that explosion, so I gave it to her, pressing my thumb to her clit and leaning over to nip at her pretty little nipples. When I bit down, she gasped, which only made me thrust harder, slamming myself into her and making her tiny bed squeak. "Gabe! Gabe!" Her breath caught as I curled my tongue along her ear and nipped again, and right then and there I had the mind-blowing pleasure of feeling Everly's pussy clamp down on my cock as I fucked her.

"Shit, baby, yes." I was babbling but I didn't care. I didn't care about anything but the fact that I was claiming this girl. She was mine, mine, *mine*.

Something white and hot exploded behind my eyeballs even as fireworks exploded up my spine. I came with a roar, thrusting into her so hard I was sure I was going to split her in half. But she clung to me, and at the perfect moment, she raked her fingers down my back, sending me over the edge into oblivion.

Chapter Twenty-Nine

EVERLY

Gabe and Beau had Rachel and I moved into our tiny little gray-shingled house in a matter of hours. That first weekend, Gabe called me and asked me out on a date.

"A date?" I squealed.

He chuckled. "A date," he repeated. "But don't come over here. I want to pick you up."

"You mean..." I put my hand to my mouth in shock.

Now he was outright laughing at me. "I can drive. I just got the okay from the doctor."

"I had no idea."

"How would you? You're my girl, not my nurse." My heart squeezed to hear him say it again. I wasn't sure I'd ever get over him calling me his girl.

He wasn't done blowing my mind. "I know a guy is supposed to pick up his girl for a date, but I'm gonna let you drive."

I narrowed my eyes. "Oh, really? Why's that?"

"You'll see. Wear something nice," he said, then hung up the phone.

My heart raced as I stared at the screen. I wanted to run through the town, shouting out the news to complete strangers. "Gabe King is taking me on a date! I'm going on a date!" I wished there was someone I could tell who would be happy for me.

Then I remembered there *was*.

I got up from my bed and went to the door of my bedroom. Rachel sat in the living room, immersed in a giant fantasy novel from the library. She looked up and smiled when she saw me. "Hey, was that Gabe?" she asked.

"Oh, sorry, was I loud?"

"I wasn't eavesdropping," she said quickly. "I'm used to filtering out the noise of people around me."

I grinned at her. We were both still so wary and careful around each other. I opened my mouth to apologize again. Instead I said, "Guess what?"

She raised her eyebrows in that quiet way she had, not using more words than absolutely necessary.

I knew her well enough now to realize that was her way of showing interest, so I barreled on in glee. "Gabe is taking me on a date! And he's driving over!"

"Oh, he's driving? That's wonderful!" she cried, clasping her hands together in a gesture of prayer. She looked down at her hands and consciously unclenched them before looking back up with her eyes shining mischievously. "A date, huh?"

"I know. I'm so secular," I teased.

"You're gonna have to tell me all about it because I have no idea what dating is," she sighed. "Where are you going?"

"No idea. Maybe a restaurant? The bar? He said to dress nice, but I don't have anything for going out. All my clothes are work clothes or scrubs. Think I should wear scrubs on my big date?"

Rachel hopped to her feet. "Absolutely not," she said, her face thunderous.

"I was just kidding."

"I know, but come with me anyway," she ordered.

Confused, I followed her into her bedroom. It was smaller than mine, but so pin-neat that it felt bigger by far. "What are you doing?" I fell into awed silence as she opened her closet door.

Dress after dress hung in Rachel's closet. Sparkly tops nestled next to scoop-necked sweaters organized by color. I leafed my fingers through the shiny, slinky fabrics, pausing to admire a gauzy blouse before whistling at a skin-tight orange Lycra dress. "Did you rob a boutique?" I gasped.

She laughed quietly. "When I first got out," she said, brushing her hand fondly across an angora sweater, "I wanted to blend in. It was easy enough to get the credit card. The hard part was knowing what real people actually wear day to day." She chuckled ruefully as she pulled out an especially bright top sewn entirely from sparkly palliates. "Turns out you guys don't wear clubwear every day of the week."

"There are still tags on most of these. You could return them."

She shook her head and ducked away from me. "If I did that, I wouldn't be able to help my friend look pretty for her date."

It felt good to grab her in a spontaneous hug and it felt even better when she hugged me back. "What do you think I should pick out? You're a little smaller than me, so maybe not a dress..."

She thumbed through the hangers with an intent look before pausing. "This one."

It was a blue tank top with a gauzy blue long-sleeved overlay that fastened with one pearly button at the chest. "It's the same color as your eyes. He'll love it." Her grin twisted into mischief again. "I don't mind if he tears it."

"You little minx!" I scolded, but I definitely wouldn't mind either.

Rachel insisted that I take her silver heels too, even though I had barely walked in heels before. A pair of dark wash jeans and a swipe of lip gloss were all it took to feel pretty. I liked that when I looked in the mirror, I still looked like me. I didn't look like someone else, like I had the night Gabe and I met. I looked like a version of myself I could be proud of.

The crunch of wheels on the gravel road was loud enough for both of us to hear, and Rachel flew to the window to check. "I think it's him?" she called, sounding confused. "I don't know his car."

"He'd probably be in his mom's SUV," I called from the bathroom as I patted water through my ponytail to combat the frizz around my hairline. Humidity was not my friend.

"It's not an SUV," Rachel called back. "It's a car." She paused. "A pretty fancy-looking car."

Curious, I met her at the window. A light blue Acura stopped in front of our house. "That's not him?" I said. "Or it might be? I don't know."

The car door opened and there was no one else it could be other than Gabe King.

It took my breath away to see him standing so straight and tall. And wow, was he tall. Standing this close to my tiny little house, he looked like he wouldn't fit inside.

He wore dark jeans that hugged his hips and renewed my belief that I was an ass-woman. His casually untucked gray button-down looked soft and comfortable. The light drizzle was beading upon his skin, which still somehow retained the traces of a tan in spite of the sun not shining for months on end.

Rachel made a small noise next to me. She was literally biting her lip as she watched Gabe stride—slowly and carefully, but still confidently—to our front door. "Are you checking out my man?" I teased.

She shook her head as if waking from a dream. "Sorry, I—" She bit her lip again. "He looks exactly like everything my church warned me about." Rachel turned and gave me a smile that was half wicked, half wistful. "Does he have any brothers?" she joked.

I laughed and was still laughing when Gabe knocked on the door. Some dating rule somewhere probably stated that I should have made him wait a couple minutes, keep him on his toes. But hell, not knowing or following the rules at all had gotten me this far—with Gabe King of the King Brothers waiting on my doorstep to take me out in his fancy car—so I didn't intend to follow them now.

I threw open the front door with such exuberance that it left a dent in the wall. "Shit," I sighed, and turned to Rachel. "I'll pay for it."

Then I threw myself into his arms.

He grunted as I slammed into him. Gabe had to step back to catch his balance, but he caught me in his arms all the same and returned my wild kiss with the same fervor. "We're going on a date!" I exhaled when I finally came up for air.

"I mean, we could stay right here," he said, his eyes darkening and his voice going all growly in the way that always made my toes tingle. “I’m sure Rachel wouldn’t mind taking a walk.”

“It’s raining,” Rachel pointed out sourly from the kitchen doorway.

I hadn’t realized she was listening and blushed a little. “No way,” I mock pouted. “You promised me a date and you also promised I’d get to drive your fancy car, so don’t try to weasel your way out of it now.”

He laughed, a full-throated belly laugh, and pulled me to him. “There you go,” he murmured into my hair. “You ask for what you want and make sure you get it, baby. That’s how you do it.” He turned to wave to Rachel. “I guess this means we’re leaving.”

“Have fun!” Rachel said. I couldn’t miss the wistful note in her voice as she closed the door behind us.

“She needs to go out, too,” I fretted. “She’s never been allowed to go out and have fun before.”

Gabe stopped and turned. “You want to invite her to come with us?”

I pressed my lips together and scrunched my nose, making him laugh again. “Good,” he said. “Let’s bring her with us next time, okay? Sound good?”

“Sounds perfect,” I agreed, slipping my arm into his. It was hard to shake the habit of holding him up a little, acting as his personal crutch, and he knew it. With a glance downward, and one perfectly raised eyebrow, he let me know that he was fine to walk on his own. I contented myself with a squeeze of his bicep, which made him laugh, and cleared my throat. “So why do you need me to drive tonight? Is your right ankle bothering you?”

“No,” he said as he held open the driver’s side door for me. I grinned at him and slid into the leather seat, smoothing my hands over the console and brushing over the space-aged dashboard. “I wanted you to see if you liked driving it.”

“Oh my god, well...it’s gonna be a wee bit different from driving Grim around, but I’ll do my best to adjust.”

“Turn it on. No, don’t press the accelerator or slip it into neutral or any of those other gyrations you usually do. Just...press the button. Right there.”

I pressed the button and the car purred smoothly to life.

"That almost felt like cheating," I whispered. "It can't be that easy."

He chuckled and gently shut the door, then came around and slid into the seat next to me. "How about you test it out a little?"

"Are you trying to make me jealous here or something? What are you up to, King?"

He shook his head with a smile that made me want to kiss him for no damn reason, but the siren song of a sexy car lured me away from his grin. I threw it into reverse. "Oh my god!" I cried as the engine hummed. "I'm sorry, Gabe. I'm leaving you for your car."

He looked like the cat who'd swallowed the canary. "Keep driving," he urged.

"Why? So I can know for sure that I want to marry a vehicle? Oh my god, you just press the accelerator and it goes! I feel *lazy*!"

"I'm glad you like it."

"You shouldn't be glad. I'm breaking up with you right now so I can have some alone time with this car."

He grinned. "What if I told you that you could have us both?"

I froze and looked at him, then remembered I was piloting a gorgeous piece of automotive engineering. I wrenched my eyes back to the road. "Have you...both?"

"This car is for you, Everly."

I swerved to the side of the road and threw it in park before I drove us both into a building. "What on earth are you saying? You didn't really buy me a car, did you, Gabe? No," I shook my head. "It's too much. I can't accept it." I unbuckled my seatbelt and reached for the door.

He stopped me with a hand on my shoulder. "I'm not giving it to you," he said. When I turned back to him, he smiled. "Come on now. I know you better than that. I knew you wouldn't accept a gift like this, so that's not what it is."

"What is it, then?"

"You need a reliable car," he said with a note of urgency in his voice. "It's not right that you had to deal with that deathtrap for so long, and I don't ever want to see you having a panic attack about it—" I ducked my head away in embarrassment. He squeezed my hand. "I don't want that to happen to you again, baby. So I figured if I could help you, I would. And I can." He reached out and patted the dash. "This car is the loaner from my Dad's friend's garage. Since it's a loaner, he's totally cool with it being loaned out indefinitely. You take it. You take care of it, fill it with gas, and make all the recommended maintenance visits." He grinned at this and wagged his finger. "Believe me, my Dad and his buddies insist on *all* of the recommended maintenance and then some." I grinned in spite of myself. "If you can take care of it, it's yours. If they need it back, which Chuck at the garage insisted they probably wouldn't, then you bring it in and they'll hook you up with another loaner." He patted the dash again. "Though I doubt it'll be as nice as this one. I made sure to snag you the good one."

"Gabe." I didn't know what to say, so I kissed him. He seemed to like that response just fine.

Chapter Thirty

GABE

The only fancy restaurant in town was also the only sit-down restaurant in town, so that's where I'd made our reservation. Jimmy's Pasta House did carbs admirably and had candles on the table. It was a far cry from the Michelin-starred places I'd eaten with the last girl in my life, but it felt right for this girl.

My girl.

The soft candlelight made her eyes sparkle as she looked over the menu. "I'm going to have to be careful," she sighed as she ran her finger down the list. "I borrowed this top from Rachel and I don't want to get sauce on it."

"Why would you get sauce on it?" I wondered, eyeing the top appreciatively. I'd have to thank Rachel when I saw her next. It matched the blue of Everly's eyes exactly.

She glanced up at me with a wry smile. "I'm a total slob when I eat. I should have brought a bib."

I gave her a quizzical look. "I find it hard to believe you're a slob."

"Just when I'm eating," she corrected, quickly catching my meaning. "I'm definitely way neater as a nurse."

I leaned back in my chair and set my menu down. "What made you want to be a nurse?" I wondered. "I know your parents have the bakery in town. You never wanted to bake?" Everly ran her tongue across her bottom teeth. "Uh oh. Sore subject?"

She shook her head. "Only to them," she said with more than a little steel in her voice. "I've known I wanted to be a nurse since I was nine years old."

I whistled softly. "That's a long time. What made you want to do it?"

She took a deep breath, like she needed to collect her thoughts, and just as she did, the smiling waitress appeared to take our order. I was happy that, in spite of her fear of being a slob, Everly still ordered a big plate of chicken parm. "That's my girl," I murmured.

When our orders had been taken, I turned back to her. "Why I wanted to be a nurse," she said softly, toying with her fork. "I know. I remembered the question."

"This sounds like a story," I prompted.

She kept twisting her fork in her fingers, her eyes a million miles away. "I was nine and my stomach really hurt." She tapped the fork against the table and looked at me, then back down to the fork. I held my breath. "I told my parents. I'm sure I did, although to this day they insist I never said a word. But it hurt so much I was doubled over in school." The corner of her mouth lifted in a wry, rueful smile. "I got in trouble for walking funny, actually."

"Jesus," I growled.

She glanced up and her smile widened until it was genuine. "It was the school nurse who finally helped me. She noticed and pulled me out of the line in the cafeteria."

"What was wrong?"

"My appendix," she said, some of that steel back in her voice. "Apparently it was hours from bursting. She noticed me and made sure I was taken care of. She even came to visit me in the hospital." Everly took a sip of her water as I tried to wrap my mind around what it must have been like for that poor, invisible girl. Clenching my fist under the table, I swore to myself that I'd notice everything about her. "I guess I developed this sort of hero worship of nurses after that," she said, sounding brighter now, her eyes shining with the opportunity to talk about the work she loved. "I built them up into superheroes with powers like X-ray vision and things like that, so of course I wanted to be just like them." Her chin jutted out a little. "My mom still insists it's my own fault for not telling her."

"It's not," I told her flatly.

She cocked her head to the side. "I know that."

I leaned forward and took her hand. "I know you know it. But I also wanted to make sure you heard it from someone else."

She lowered her eyes, her lashes casting shadows over her cheekbones. I held my breath and squeezed her hand.

Everly stood up. I was already sliding my chair back to meet her when she took my face in her hands. I met her kiss with everything I had, forgetting the restaurant and the people in the tables around us. It was so easy to lose myself in this girl. I was addicted to her fire and the hell-bent way she kissed me.

When she pulled back, breathing hard, the whole restaurant was silent. Our waitress stood there, stock still, with our meals on her tray. From over in the corner came a slow, sarcastic round of applause.

Everly ducked back down to her seat, but I stood up straight and proud and waved, like I had to countless audiences before.

Then I heard Everly swear. "You okay?" I whispered and sat back down again. I expected her to complain about being the center of attention and I wanted to remind her that that was one of the perks of being my girl.

"Yeah," she complained, dipping her napkin in her water glass. "But I just got fucking tomato sauce on Rachel's shirt."

I clapped my hands and pressed my fingertips to my lips. "You're fucking spectacular," I told her. "Where'd I find you?"

She lifted her chin, proud in spite of the wet mark above her left breast. "Right under here," she teased, touching the tip of my nose.

Chapter Thirty-One

EVERLY

The next week, it was finally warm enough at night to sleep with the windows open. I'd been looking forward to this since Rachel and I moved in to the little gray house. It seemed so nice in theory to lie in bed listening to the burble of the creek.

But the creek wasn't burbling. It was roaring.

Weeks of rain had left it swollen and fast moving. There was flooding in the low-lying areas north of town, where Rachel and I lived, and the rain was still falling. Lying here listening to the rushing waters wasn't soothing, it was nerve-wracking.

The din had my nerves jangling. I took a deep breath and counted backwards by sevens from three hundred—a trick that had always worked in the past—but was still awake when I got to negative one. I contemplated going further into the negatives, but realized that the debate itself was keeping me awake. Worse, my hands were shaking.

Just a little. The slightest tremor. But it had been weeks since my last attack, and I didn't want to let them get any worse. I needed a distraction. The noise of the creek and the dark of the house had the strange effect of making me feel like the only person in the world.

I thought about getting up and seeing if Rachel was having the same trouble sleeping, but my roommate's shy conversation wasn't what I needed.

I grabbed my phone.

Me: I can't sleep.

The reply came almost immediately.

Gabe: What do you need, baby?

Me: I think...

Me: You, maybe.

He sent back a smiley face.

Gabe: Wait. Maybe?

Me: Sorry. Definitely is a better word.

Gabe: Yes it is. I can come over.

I licked my lips. The thought was appealing enough to make my hands still, but...

Me: You wouldn't fit in my bed.

Gabe: We made it work before.

Me: You're dirty.

Gabe: I know. But you're right. Your bed is too tiny and mine is huge.

Me: ?

Me: No it isn't, that hospital bed is even worse than mine.

Gabe: See now, this is why it sucks you're not my nurse anymore...

Me: You want to go back to acting professionally?

Gabe: Slow down. I never said that.

I sent him a laughing face emoji. Even texting with him made me feel better, and I usually hated texting.

Gabe: What I was trying to say was that the hospital bed got picked up today.

Me: Really????

Gabe: I'm lying in a real bed right now.

Gabe: After all that time in a tiny hospital bed, it almost feels TOO big, you know?

Gabe: Plenty of room to share.

I stood up and grabbed the keys to the Acura off my bedside table. Then I thought for a second.

Me: You never took back your key, you know.

Gabe: Oh, I know.

I grinned at my screen.

Gabe: But I'll meet you at the back door anyway.

Driving through the dark country roads around Crown Creek had always given me the heebie-jeebies before. All those dark trees and dark houses looming made me feel like I was floating in space. But since I was going to Gabe, the night seemed soft and friendly. Even the misting rain was warm on my face as I walked around to the back of the Kings' house and climbed up onto the deck.

He was waiting, like he'd said, and seeing him standing there straight and tall, healed and whole, made my heart lurch.

I went to him and when he kissed me the tremor in my hands had nothing to do with panic and everything to do with all the feelings I had for him. He made love to me slowly, luxuriating in the huge expanse of the bed, bringing me to the brink again and again until I was completely spent and sated.

Afterward, after he'd brought me a warm cloth to clean myself, and laughed about how it was his turn to give me a sponge bath, he folded his huge body around mine.

"Are you okay?" I whispered in the dark. His body was so warm and his expert fucking had worn me out so thoroughly that I was almost asleep before he answered. "I'm fucking perfect."

I laid there, listening to his breathing, and tried to piece together the past couple weeks. How we'd found each other again after that lost night. How one filthy kiss had seared me into his heart so completely that he'd recognized me from its power. I giggled a little at how absurd it was and he snuffled awake. "What's funny, baby?"

"I feel like Cinderella. Only instead of putting a slipper on my foot to find me, you put your tongue in my mouth."

He rolled onto his back and laughed a silent, bed-shaking laugh. Grinning, I rolled over and brushed my hand up his chest, cupping it as I always did, right over his heart. "It's true," I murmured sleepily.

"I love that you thought that." He brushed my hair back from my forehead. "In fact, I think I love *you*."

My chest hitched for only a second before I smiled and turned to kiss his chest. “Good,” I murmured. “Because I love you.”

He brushed his hand over my forehead again, and then again, stroking me gently with his fingertips. I fell asleep listening to his heartbeat.

Chapter Thirty-Two

GABE

I loved her. I knew that much for certain.

I was uncertain about everything else.

Kit Lomber called that very morning, right as Everly was slipping out the back door to go home to her new house. I held my phone in my hand, praying he'd call right back as soon as I kissed her goodbye.

He did. "Gabriel!" he shouted into my ear after I'd said hello.

"Mr. Lomber—"

"Told you ages ago, call me Kit. Mr. Lomber is my dad!" Kit was old enough to actually *be* my dad, but he didn't like it when I reminded him of that fact.

"Right, Kit. How's it going?"

"That's the question I should be asking you, isn't it?" he boomed. "We've got almost the whole crew ready and on stand-by. Location scouts are out doing their thing. The only thing that's up in the air right now is when the star of the show is gonna be ready to start filming."

I swallowed and hurried up the stairs to my room, shutting the door behind me. This felt like a call I needed to have in private, but I realized I'd made a mistake in coming back up here the second I glanced at the bed.

The bed, rumpled from a night spent loving Everly.

Even when I closed my eyes, I could see it. It was burned into my retinas like an afterimage of the sun. "Um," was all I could say to Kit.

"You're on the mend for sure," he said. "I can hear it in your voice. You sound much stronger."

"Yeah," I wavered. "I'm doing better." That rumpled bed was like an accusing finger pointed in my face.

"Gabe, level with me." When Kit called me by my nickname, that was when things got serious. His buddy-buddy-heart-to-heart chats set my teeth on edge on a good day, and today, in spite of how it had started, was turning out to not be a very good day. "I'm hearing a lot of hesitation here," he went on. "I understand if you want to take a step back. You've earned it. But—and correct me if I'm not remembering this right—I distinctly recall you telling me you were excited to come back to the show. You told me that you—hang on, I wrote this down because I thought it'd make a great tagline for the season. You told me, 'I almost died. Now I'm ready to really start living.'"

I sucked in my breath to hear my own arrogant words read back to me. I'd said them when I was stuck in the sunroom, confined to the hospital bed. I'd called Kit, practically begging him to set a date for me to return, and I even started marking the days off on a pad of paper like a convict marks the prison wall. Those were dark days.

My days were full of light now.

"I said that," I exhaled. "I remember."

"So level with me, buddy. Why the hesitation? Are you still hurting? I don't want you pushing yourself to heal too fast. You know we expect you to be back in top physical condition once we start filming."

Right then and there, he gave me an out. I could buy myself some time to figure out what the hell came next.

And to figure out if Everly loving me meant I could convince her to come along for the ride.

I let myself think that nice thought for only a moment before I pushed it from my brain. Like hell Everly would leave with me. She had school and her work, and she'd rented that house with Rachel. I loved that she was building a life on her terms. What right did I have to make her live it on mine?

I sucked in another deep breath and tried to pitch my voice as melancholy. "It's pretty much exactly that, Kit," I sighed. "I overdid it in physical therapy—trying so hard to get back into top physical condition, you know—and I fucked up my ankle." This was all true. He didn't need to know that I was describing something that happened weeks ago. "I'm limping pretty bad, buddy, and I need—"

"More time. I hear you." I could imagine him nodding gravely. "Well, Gabe, I'm disappointed, but I can't say I'm surprised. Luckily you've got a magician like me on your side." His casual boasting made me grin in exasperation. "I'll take care of smoothing out schedules, but you gotta do something for me."

"Yeah, sure," I said automatically.

"You gotta give me a date."

"A date?" I stalled.

"Right. A concrete date I can give them so we don't mess with the crew's schedules like this again. Give me the date you're gonna be all healed up and ready to go."

I paced in a tight circle, feeling trapped. A concrete date? "Um... give me a month."

Kit *tsked*. "Damn, buddy. You're really putting me in a bind here. I can do two weeks?"

"A month," I insisted. "Give me a solid month to heal up."

"That puts us out to the twenty-fourth? That's a Sunday. I'll send the plane for you on that Friday the twenty-second." There was a curt finality in his voice. "I'll let the crew know."

"Thanks," I said.

But he had already hung up.

"Fuck!" I shouted and hurled my phone at the rumpled bed. That was twenty-eight days. Twenty-eight days with Everly before I handed her a bomb and asked her to be happy about it.

The way I figured it, I had two options. I could tell her right now, give her time to prepare, and run the risk of her breaking things off with me prematurely. What sane girl wanted to go steady with a time limit?

My other option was to keep quiet as long as I could and let us both enjoy the time we had left without worrying about the future. Of course, if I did that, I ran the risk of her hating me for not giving her a choice.

Funny how neither risk was one I wanted to take.

That night, when I called Everly after her shift, she apologized about not being able to hang out. "Remember I told you I wanted to take Rachel out?" she said as my heart fell. "That was tonight. I definitely told you, right?"

I blew out an explosive sigh. "Yeah, baby, you did," I promised her.

"I can cancel," she offered. "You sound weird. What's up?"

The last thing I needed was to stay home tonight. After Kit's call, I'd paced around the house so much that Beau got all concerned and Finn started throwing things at me. Spending the night without my girl seemed too much to ask. "I'm fine," I told her. "I'm just feeling cooped up."

"You know, we'd love to have you come out, but..." Her voice trailed off.

"But?" I prompted.

She gave a nervous laugh. "I've sort of built up the wonders of alcohol to the point where Rachel is insisting I take her to a bar. She's in her room getting ready right now." Everly dropped her voice conspiratorially. "You know, for a girl who spent her life dressed in what amounts to a burlap sack, she's got amazing fashion sense."

I wasn't thinking about Rachel. I was still stuck on what she'd said before. "You're headed to a bar? Which one?"

"Crown Tavern, of course. Is there any other decent bar in this town?"

"You mean..." Now it was my turn to drop my voice. "The place where we met."

She made a little "oh" sound. "Shit, Gabe, I guess I figured that—"

"No, I know, baby. I know." Inside I was practically vibrating with the idea of it. To sit at the table with them while they drank was a huge risk to my sobriety.

It was exactly the kind of risk I needed right now. One I knew I could take and win. "If it's okay with you, I'd still love to come out. Someone's got to take care of you two naughty girls."

She laughed. "Please. A wallflower and a girl who recently escaped a cult? Naughty is not the word I'd use." Then her voice took on a distinctly naughty tone. "You know I want to see you," she purred. "But it's not fair to make Rachel be a third wheel."

"I'll bring someone for her," I interjected.

"Who?"

"I've got way too many brothers. You pick."

"Hmm. She already met Beau the day you guys helped us move, so she might be more comfortable with him versus Finn, who's a bit—"

"Of a prickly asshole," I finished. "You got it. I'll meet you there."

I hung up the phone, feeling that buzzy excitement again. Maybe it wasn't jumping out of an airplane, but it was a risk all the same. A tiny one. One I could totally handle, especially with Everly there.

Chapter Thirty-Three

EVERLY

Something wasn't right.

It started the night he and Beau met Rachel and me at the Crown Tavern. The four of us had had a lot of fun, and Beau and Rachel hit it off, their shared quiet intensity shutting Gabe and I out enough that we felt free to kiss and flirt all night. He handled being around alcohol beautifully; making sure to keep an eye on our drinks when we went to the bathroom and giving all four of us a safe ride home.

But then he wanted to do it again.

And again.

I was trying very, *very* hard to be okay with it.

But then there was the other day, when he jumped off the second step of the porch. He'd landed with his fist in the air, but my heart was in my throat. "What the hell do you think you're doing?" I shouted before I could stop myself. "Are you insane?"

He'd looked it. That was the thing. His eyes were lit with this unnatural light, and as we left for our date he'd driven way too fast along the winding road next to the creek. I'd tried like hell not to yell at him again, but when my hands started shaking, I'd exploded at him, demanding to know why he was putting us both at risk. "An adrenaline junkie is just another kind of junkie!" I'd shouted.

He'd dropped me off early that night and set a new record for time going by before he called me again. "I shouldn't have put you at risk like that," he'd said softly. But even as I accepted his apology, I noticed he'd said nothing about risking himself.

Now I was looking at my phone and wondering how I felt about the voicemail I'd just gotten from Rachel. "Hey Ever, I wanted to let you know that Beau and I were going out tonight. And, uh, the weird thing...is that Gabe is coming with us? Yeah, I know, but he says he'll just hang out and be our designated driver, which is really nice and all, but I sort of feel weird about it. So if you're around, swing by the tavern and hang out with us so he's got someone with him, okay? We're getting there around nine."

I let my hand drop. "What the fuck are you doing, Gabe?" I muttered aloud.

"How are you doing, Beverly?" the head nurse on the floor where I was doing my rotation called. "Everything okay?"

I shook my head to clear it. "Just fine!" I called, scurrying past her before I turned back and smiled sweetly. "It's Everly, by the way. I know. My sister's name is Abriella. My parents are allergic to consonants."

She burst out laughing, which made me feel better about correcting her, but it didn't do anything about the pit in my stomach that Gabe's odd behavior had opened up.

Without meaning to, I flashed back to the night he'd told me about his addictions. "It wasn't my fault," he'd claimed.

I knew enough about recovery to know that taking responsibility was a huge part of it. If he didn't feel responsible for using in the first place, then nothing was stopping him from falling victim to it again.

I shuddered and shoved that thought out of my mind. If he was using again, I'd know.

Then again, my workload had been insane these past couple weeks. We'd only been able to snatch a few nights out together, and one of them we spent fighting over his risk-taking.

I liked to think I'd know, but could I be certain?

That thought haunted me as I hurried through my rounds. I needed to know for certain that Gabe wasn't using again. If he was, I needed to get him help. If he wasn't, then I needed to find out what else was going on. My anxious mind raced through scenarios that made my hands shake so bad I nearly dropped a bedpan. If I didn't do something to head off these nerves, I was going to have an attack. I could feel it.

That clinched it. My rotation ended at nine. If I raced home, I'd have enough time to change and put on one of Rachel's fancy tops. Then I could head over to the Crown and figure out what the hell was going on with the man I loved.

I rolled up to the tavern feeling full of hope. Whatever was going on, I knew we were strong enough to get through it. Our connection was stronger than this. It was strong enough to withstand anything. I knew that.

That's why I wasn't suspicious when I walked in and spotted him by the bar, leaning in to the blonde girl sitting next to him. Sure, her hair was the most perfect shade of sunny blonde I had ever seen, and her turned-up nose made my huge schnoz look like an elephant's trunk, but I wasn't scared about her at all until I walked up to them without them noticing me.

Until I heard him say her name.

Noelle.

He was talking—closely, intimately—to Noelle. The girl he'd once loved enough to propose to. The beautiful pop star who'd snared his heart so thoroughly, their break-up had also broken up his band.

And he had no idea I was even in the room.

Chapter Thirty-Four

GABE

Why was I at the bar? Beau and Rachel didn't want me there. I missed Everly. And sitting in a bar surrounded by drunk people while nursing a Coke was getting really old.

I shouldn't have come. I needed to leave. I was in the middle of standing up to tell that to Beau when it happened.

I saw a fucking ghost.

She floated in with her head held high, but I knew her and I could see the panic underneath her polished facade. She gave the whole place a practiced sweep of her eyes.

Like she was used to casing the joint.

Like she'd been at this for a while.

I stood stock still and stared. Had someone spiked my drink? Beau's dangerous rumble broke into my thoughts. "Oh, what the fuck..."

"So she is here," I muttered to him under my breath. "I'm not imagining this?"

"She's here," my brother said in a voice I'd never heard from him before. "And I think she sees you."

She did. It was momentarily gratifying to see that she looked just as shocked to find me as I was to be found.

"Gabe," she called.

I cleared my throat. "Noelle."

It made no sense that she was here. My mind insisted this wasn't happening even as she leaped into my arms, throwing herself around my neck. I'm not a complete asshole. I caught her so she wouldn't go slamming to the ground. But I immediately put her back down and stepped back. "What the hell do you think you're doing?" I hissed.

I'd watched her new video and been proud of how I'd felt nothing. But *watching* her didn't compare at all to the tornado of emotions that came from *seeing* her.

And *remembering*.

She spoke in that little pouty, breathless voice she'd always use to cajole me. "I heard you were hurt."

"I'm better now." I folded my arms across my chest.

This bothered her. "I see that," she said softly. "I wanted to come earlier."

I snorted. "It's okay, Noelle. You don't have to lie."

She pressed her lips together. "Then I *should* have come earlier." It sounded like she was trying to apologize.

This was a surprise. I had never known Noelle to admit fault. Ever. And that made me wary. "Okay."

"Gabe?"

Fuck. "Noelle, I really don't know why you're here, but..."

"I'm here because I've missed you," she interrupted smoothly.

Beau swore under his breath. I shook my head at her. "No," I said firmly. "This isn't happening. You need to get the fuck out of my bar. My town. Get the fuck out of my whole state, Noelle. I'm serious."

The tears and hysterics I braced for never came. She looked the same, but something about her had fundamentally changed. A layer of artifice had been stripped away. There was strength and wariness in those blue eyes that hadn't been there before, and something wounded cowered under her skin.

She turned her palms up in a gesture of surrender. "I need to tell you something."

"I don't want to hear excuses and I don't want you to tell me you can explain." My blood was heating up. "There's no way you could explain how you said you loved me and then turned around and had Bennett's cock in your mouth."

She winced and glanced over at Beau, who stared at her implacably. Rachel had her hand over her mouth. Noelle reddened. "Gabe, can we go somewhere and talk in private?"

I took three big steps to the left and leaned against the bar. "This works for me," I said. "Go ahead. Talk."

Keeping her head held high, she turned and looked at my brother. "It's good to see you again, Beau. I've missed you guys."

Beau stayed silent, but the set of his jaw didn't change He had my back and if I called on him, he'd be there for me in whatever way I needed.

In a way, I was impressed with Noelle's guts right now. She'd come to my home turf. She had to know she'd be outnumbered. She was here anyway.

"Okay," she said, sitting down on a barstool. "Thank you for letting me talk." Then she turned and looked me full in the eye. "I'm not going to lie to you and tell you you didn't see what you saw."

This wasn't what I was expecting. I was ready for a fight. I itched to make her feel half as shitty as I'd felt the day she betrayed me. Her clear-eyed admission made a lump form in my throat. "Okay," I said, consciously unclenching my fist.

Noelle watched my hand. She took a deep breath and looked straight ahead. Not meeting my eyes seemed to make the words come a little easier. "You saw what you saw. I was doing what you saw me doing. But I didn't want it."

For the second time this minute I felt like she'd punched me in the gut. "What?" My eyelid twitched. "He was forcing you?" I didn't love her anymore, but I would kill him for this without hesitating.

She darted a frightened look at me. "No, not like that. It wasn't..." She swallowed. "Rape?" The word came out like a question. "Not exactly."

"I don't get it."

"Clearly, I don't either." Her laugh was nothing like the high, breathless sound she used to make when we were together. Was I hearing her real laugh now? Was this clear-eyed, frank-talking woman the real Noelle St. Lucia?

Who was it that I had been in love with? Was she a dream I'd made up in my head? This bitter woman laughing ruefully as she blew out a resigned sigh was nothing like the carefree girl who'd made me feel like I was drunk. "It started out as a 'I scratch your back you scratch mine' sort of deal," she said, darting another glance at me. "Literally. He liked it when I scratched his back."

"Fucking gross."

"I know." She heaved a sigh. "But I told myself it was fine. A little weird, but what was it compared with what he could do for me?" She shook her head and shot a grateful glance to the bartender for setting a wineglass in front of her. She gulped it like a frat boy doing a funnel and went on. "He was this paunchy, middle-aged loser, you know? He was always telling me how beautiful I was, how I was this goddess who was gracing him with my presence." She laughed, a bitter, acid sound. "He let me think that I was the one who was using him."

As if fortified by the wine, she looked at me full on. "You remember how he set us up?"

I nodded tightly, not trusting my voice to say anything aloud.

She drained her glass. "Before I met you, he coached me. Told me all the wonderful things you could do for my career. Being with you was the shot in the arm I needed, for visibility," she confessed.

"Fuck," I hissed. Jonah had always accused her of that very thing. Using me. Lost in love, I'd refused to believe him.

Her hand brushed my arm. "No, Gabe," she said, as if she could read my thoughts. "It wasn't like that. I did love you. Oh my god, I loved you so much. But the more in love I fell, the more jealous Bennett got. He held it over me, threatening my career, all the work I'd done, the contacts he'd made for me, the deals he'd cut. He'd pull them all if I didn't keep him happy. So I had to...keep him happy." She glanced at her wine glass again, but it was empty. "First it was the back scratching, then it was...kisses. Then..." She looked disgusted. "I showed him my breasts once after a particularly nasty blowout. And the first time I...I..." She took a shuddering breath. "The first time I gave him oral was when we got back from the island." She shook her head. "He was jealous, I think. Mad that I got away from him. He told me that my album had stalled." The bartender brought her another glass of wine and she clutched it gratefully. "You remember how hard I was pushing you for the duet?"

"Yes," I said. Regret turned somersaults in my belly. I was torn between disgust at her and disgust at myself for being so far up my own ass that I didn't see how she'd been wrenched around like this.

"It was the only thing I could think of to get free of him. I thought that if I was on your album, I'd make my name. And...and I thought maybe if we were able to spend more time together, stuck in a studio and everything, you'd be able to keep me safe from him."

"Fucking hell, Noelle." The world slanted sideways, and I gripped the bar tightly to keep from sliding with it. "Why didn't you tell me?"

She threw up her hands in helpless surrender. "What was I going to say? That I'd been cheating on you since the moment we met? I thought I could control it when it started. Bennett—you know how he was, acting like he was your friend, wanting to fit in. He'd get these puppy-dog eyes when he thought we were ignoring him. He was always saying he should get more credit for getting us together, asking for hugs. Telling me how nice he was being. He made me feel like it was always my choice. Saying we had to work together, look out for each other. The more attention I gave him, the harder he worked for me. The first time he kissed me he tried to play it off for laughs, like it was an accident. I felt like maybe I'd misinterpreted, and you didn't say or do anything so I thought I'd imagined it. I used my body. It was part of what I did. I got the results I wanted, right? The first time he put my hand on his dick, I wanted to go to you right then and there. But he reminded me that I was in a bind. I was touring with you. If I told, I'd lose my allowance. And I'd already put my career on hold for you."

"I never asked you to." Guilt made me sound sullen.

"You wanted me there, Gabe. You always said how I was the only thing that made you feel alive during the touring. The only thing that made sense. What else was I supposed to think other than you needed me?"

I knew I would sound like a prick but I said it anyway. "You needed me more."

"Of course I did." She admitted it readily. "I was using you and I'll never forgive myself for not loving you the way I should have. I know that now. But I have always loved you."

I tried to look back and see her loving me. "All I remember is 'Gabe get me on the record, Gabe buy this for me, Gabe talk to Bennett for me.' Seems like you could have done some talking to Bennett yourself."

"I felt like I started out as a lion tamer, but the lion turned around and ate me alive. I didn't want to have sex with him."

"Did he force you?"

"I never said no. But I never said yes, either. I thought I had to. To have a career. To stay close to you. I thought I was doing something that would get me something in return, and all I got was losing you."

Tears streamed down her face. I had loved her. I'd wake up next to her and think she was the prettiest thing in the world. I'd loved her like a drowning man loves a life preserver, but I couldn't remember a single thing I loved about her other than how she made me feel.

I loved Everly for who she was, not what she did for me. I loved her fierce scowls and her amazing strength. I loved how fucking smart she was and how she forced me to be smart, too. I loved how she never complained, how she took everything in stride. I loved what a fucking wildcat she was in bed, and I wanted to be with her right now.

I stood up. Painfully and slowly, but I stood up. "Noelle."

She shook her head, trying to head me off before I could say anything more. "I want you to know that I'm free of him." She turned to me. "He trapped us both, in a way. You got free of the pills he hooked you on." She grabbed my hand before I could snatch it away. "I heard you went to rehab. I followed the news about you and I'm so proud of you. You're free of him and now so am I."

I was numb. Shell-shocked. "You are?" I asked dully.

She sipped her wine, her composure returning. "I don't care anymore," she declared. "I released the song without his backing. The money is mine and I'm using it to sue to get out of all my contracts." She took a deep breath. "And that's why I came back."

"That's why?"

"I'm free." She leaned forward, so close I could tell that she still used her same shampoo. "For the first time since you've known me, I am not beholden to anyone but myself." She brushed her hand along her side. "This is me. The real me. And I *miss* you, Gabe." A bright, fierce light danced in her eyes. "I miss us, and more than that, I miss what we could have been." She slipped her palm into mine. "I want to start over again. The two of us. I want to have something real with you."

"Noelle." My tongue was thick.

"Please don't say no, Gabe." Her voice caught. Noelle had cried plenty of times when we were together, but for the first time I understood that these were her real tears. "Please don't leave again. When you walked away without letting me explain, I wanted to die. I knew how badly I'd hurt you, and I am so sorry."

"I'm sorry," I said, standing up. She shook her head, a mute no no no, and my heart wanted to leap from my chest. "Noelle, I want you to know I'm sorry too. For not keeping you safe when I should have."

"Gabe. Gabe, please."

I swallowed. The hurt from seeing her like that burned like fire, even years later. But her words hadn't extinguished the blaze. Everly had.

I touched her hand, wondering if there was anything there at all, and when I had her little wrist closed in my fingers I felt it.

Nothing.

"Noelle, I am sorry—"

Her shoulders slumped.

"—but I don't love you."

"Gabe."

"No." I shook my head. "Thank you for giving me closure. Thank you for coming all this way to check on me." I felt the corner of my mouth tug a little. "I always did wonder how you'd look in Crown Creek."

She was crying freely, but she had a proud lift to her chin when she spoke. "How do I look?"

"Out of place," I said. "This isn't the place for you. I'm not the guy for you, either."

"You always wanted me to come to Crown Creek. I came."

"You came. I'm sorry, Noelle."

"Where am I going to go, Gabe?"

"You're smarter and stronger than you realize. You can go anywhere and you'll be a huge success. You don't need to ride my coattails, and you don't need to listen to Bennett's lies. You can do it yourself, okay?"

She sobbed and sagged into my arms. Her tears soaked my shirt as I held her stiffly but gently. As she cried, I made a list in my head of how I could help her, how we could take down Bennett together...but that would only give her false hope.

The only way she'd be free of Bennett was to be free of me as well.

"You're okay," I told her, patting her gently. "You're going to be just fine."

She pulled back and smiled at me, wiping away her tears. I gave her an encouraging nod and then, out of habit, out of friendship, I reached up and brushed away a piece of hair that was sticking to her face.

That's when I caught sight of Everly, standing behind Noelle, face white.

How long had she been there? Did she see us fighting?

Or had she only walked in during the embrace? Did she only see the moment I reached out and tenderly touched my ex's face?

"Everly." I stepped around Noelle and went to her. "You're here. I thought you had your rotation tonight." Fuck, why did I say it like that? It only made me sound guilty.

"Gabe?" Noelle spoke up at the worst fucking time.

"We're done now," I snapped at her over my shoulder.

Her face, which had looked calm and peaceful, crumpled. Fuck. I was fucking this all up. "Beau!" I called. "Can you take Noelle..."

My brother moved, but it was too late. Everly had heard me. "So that's Noelle," she said. Her lips were completely bloodless and her hands shook. She looked on the verge of an attack.

"Baby, no. It was nothing," I soothed. "I mean, yes. That was Noelle, but she just showed up tonight. I had no idea—" Everything I said made me sound more like a cheating fucker. "Everly, baby, I love you."

Her eyes glazed over. She hadn't heard me. She was looking over at Noelle, staring, even, and as she did I watched my girl shut down. "I'm such a fucking idiot. You've been acting so weird, but I—" Her hands went to her mouth. "You guys were together when you were using, right?"

"Right, but that has nothing to do with—"

"It makes sense," she said faintly. Her eyes flicked back up to me. Then she lifted a proud chin. "Liar," she hissed, and made for the door.

Chapter Thirty-Five

EVERLY

It made sense. It all made sense. His stupid danger-junkie risks, the distance I'd felt from him.

I kept staring, freezing up. My brain wouldn't work properly and my hands, my fucking hands, shook. If I didn't get out of here, I was going to break down and have a full-on attack right in front of his perfect ex.

I ran for the door and yanked it open. The rain poured down in huge, lashing sheets that soaked me to the skin in a matter of moments. But I felt nothing. I was numb.

Which was why I didn't feel his hand on my arm until he yanked me back to him. "Everly!"

"Get your hands off me!" Shock at how roughly he was holding me made me shout. "Who the fuck do you think you are?"

"I'm trying to tell you it was nothing. It's not what you're thinking, okay? Nothing happened. She just came here. Fucking blindsided me."

"I know what that's like!" I yelled in his face.

"I was wrong about what happened." His fingers loosened and his eyes drifted away from mine. He went somewhere inside of him. "With her. I had it all wrong."

The tenderness in his voice hurt the most. The sympathy for this woman who had supposedly stomped on his heart. How could he sound like this if he...

If he...

I almost choked on my tongue. "You still love her."

He snapped back to me. "That's not true."

"Jesus fucking Christ, Gabe, why are you jerking me around like this? Be a normal guy for once!"

He looked pissed. "I thought you understood. I'm not normal at all. I thought we cleared that up."

"Right." I crossed my arms over my chest, hugging myself. I was freezing, but I wasn't going to give him the satisfaction of seeing me shiver. I wasn't going to let him see me as fragile and needing help. He was going to see me as I was.

Fucking *livid.*

"Right," I said again. "It's quite clear. You're a danger junkie who gets off on stringing along the girl next door while secretly meeting with his famous ex. Was I just a way for you to feel like you were getting away with something? Did telling me you loved me raise the stakes high enough for you to get off on your little game?"

"Christ, Everly, cut the shit! You're spinning out."

"No, it all makes sense."

"For the fucking millionth time, *you've got it all wrong."*

"Really? Tell me everything is okay, then. Tell me you haven't been pulling away from me. Tell me you haven't been taking stupid risks these past few weeks. Tell me I'm wrong about that."

His nostrils flared. "I'm not fucking cheating on you with fucking Noelle. Christ, you know how I feel about her."

"You just told me you were wrong about her," I pointed out.

He clapped his hands over his face and dragged them down, distorting his beautiful face into a tragedy mask. "You refuse to accept a single thing I'm telling you, so how the fuck am I supposed to tell you everything is okay?"

His words hit me like a punch in the gut. "So we're not okay?"

"I'd say fucking not!" he exploded. "Jesus, with this hellacious night —you know, Everly, you knew who I was from the beginning. Unlike you, I never hid my identity. I've been open from the beginning." I took a step back, stung. He threw up his hands. "Yeah! I am who I am and if you can't handle it, go find someone else. Someone *normal*."

I couldn't get a full breath in my lungs. I was not going to have a panic attack, dear god not here, not like this. "You don't mean that," I pleaded. I wanted to take it all back. I was scared. I was hurt. I was— "You don't mean that."

He waved his hands, looking for all the world like he was washing them of me. Of us. "Yeah. I do." His voice was hollow, empty. "Go home. Study. Pass your boards. Go live your life. Be normal, Everly. Without me."

Chapter Thirty-Six

EVERLY

One strange side effect of Gabe breaking up with me was the effect it had on Rachel.

She tiptoed around me, making as little noise as possible. I kept finding little gifts in the house—a new mug for my coffee, a new shirt hanging in my closet. But it didn't feel like sweet kindnesses from a friend. It felt like desperation, and it finally pulled me out of the self-indulgent haze I'd been living in. "Hey," I said, knocking on her doorframe. "You okay?"

She leaped off her bed. "Are you?" There was panic in her eyes, though I had no idea why.

"I'm getting there," I sighed. I shook myself back out of the melancholy. "You're being jumpy as hell. What's going on?"

"I want to be sure you're going to be okay."

"I'm a big girl, Rachel."

"Of course I know that, but I thought, after a big change like this, you might want to...maybe you'd go back to your family and—"

It slowly dawned on me what she was worried about. "Rach, I'm not going to move back home again."

She exhaled a tiny, quick breath. Then the corner of her mouth twitched. "In my church, when a man sends a woman away, she returns to her family. I have to remember that's not how it's done out here."

"Gabe didn't send me away," I huffed. "He dumped me."

Rachel gave me a helpless shrug. "It's sort of the same thing," she sighed. A wave of sadness washed over her face and I realized how much about her I still didn't know. But she mastered it and pulled herself visibly back under control. "Remember," she said reprovingly. "I was there. Gabe was telling the truth when he said nothing happened. Every time that girl tried to touch him, he pulled away."

I blinked and stared up at the ceiling. The tears fell anyway. "I know. I believe him. I was only mad for a second, but that second messed everything up." Rachel gave me a sympathetic shoulder squeeze and I reached up to press my hand on hers. "He just dumped me. Just gave up. I—I never thought he'd let me go so easily."

Rachel made a sound, but didn't say anything.

I shrugged. "I don't know whether to beg him to take me back or tell him to go fuck himself." I stood up straighter. "Maybe I'll flip a coin."

"Just relax for now," Rachel said, moving into the kitchen. "I'll make us some dinner." She busily opened cupboards, but peered into each one with a frown. "Oh, goodness. We're out of everything."

"Okay," I said, heading over to the door to grab my shoes. "I'll go do a grocery run."

"Are you sure you're up to it?"

I couldn't help but grin. "Rach, you've been waiting on me hand and foot this past week. You need a break."

I grabbed my purse and headed outside, consciously swerving around the Acura and heading to Grim. I assumed Chuck from the garage would be by to pick up his loaner soon. I slid behind Grim's wheel and started him up, feeling a pang when he started smoothly. Gabe had been so good to me. How could he drop us like that?

In the five minutes it took to get into town, I swung from sadness to anger. Anger at myself for not believing him. For falling back into the old habit of assuming no one noticed me. Anger at him for giving up. Like he'd been looking for a reason to end it, and my foolish jealousy had given him the out he needed.

That thought struck me like a boot to the chest, doubling me over so that I needed the handle on the shopping cart to stay upright. He'd jumped to the worst-case scenario far too quickly for that to have been the first time he'd thought of it. I stood in the produce section, blinking at a mound of broccoli as everything slowly fell into place. His distance. Going out to bars without me. The stupid risks to piss me off and start a fight. He'd been angling for a way out and like an idiot I'd walked right into it.

I felt so low that it made sense to see her there, only five feet away from me. Her shining blonde hair, her startlingly pretty face. Of course. Of *course* Noelle St. Lucia was right here in Royal Groceries almost a week later. Why not?

She stiffened when she became aware of a person staring at her and looked up slowly. Then she executed a perfect double take. "You're Gabe's—"

"Not anymore," I finished for her.

Her mouth fell open like she was about to say something, but she caught herself and looked down. "I'm sorry to hear that," she said formally.

Of all the absurd things that had happened in my life, running into my ex's famous ex in the produce section of a small-town grocery store had to be the strangest. "What are you doing here?"

She sighed and smiled, and it was so arresting that I almost smiled with her. "I...I didn't think I'd find him so quickly, so I booked a place for..." She glanced up at me with a new light in her eyes. "You said you guys aren't together anymore?"

Hot anger spilled into my veins. "Yeah. I hear the same about you guys," I snapped.

"I'm sorry," she said quickly. "That was a bitchy thing to ask."

I studied her. She was everything I'd ever taught myself to hate and resent, but I couldn't muster those feelings about her. Not when she looked so sad. As I watched, a tear slipped silently down her cheek and she sniffed.

I took a deep breath. Then reached into my purse.

When I handed her the tissue, she seemed startled by it, like she thought I might be handing her a live scorpion or something.

"You need to move on," I said.

She looked up sharply. "You have no idea what—"

"No, I don't," I interrupted. "But I know Gabe, or at least I thought I did. And right now, all I want to do is to tell you to back off because he's mine, but he's not. Not anymore. So maybe I'm telling you to move on because I need to do the same thing."

Noelle nodded and let out a long, angry sigh. "I'm still hanging around here. How pathetic is that? I actually thought maybe I'd run into him here, or maybe one of his brothers." She pinched the bridge of her nose between her thumb and forefinger. "It figures I'd run into you."

I sniffed in amusement. "When I saw you here, I figured it was about right for how my week was going."

Her smile was tired. "I'm not a bad person, you know. I came here because when he was hurt I was halfway around the world on tour and I couldn't get away until now. I wanted to come so much sooner. I had visions of helping him, you know? Driving him around." Her mouth twisted into a leer. "Giving him sponge baths."

"I did that," I said, a possessive heat burning in my gut. "I nursed him and helped him and in return he helped me."

"But now you're not together anymore?" She sounded genuinely surprised. And more than a little concerned.

I caught her gaze. "No. But that's not your fault." Her shoulders slumped a fraction in relief as I went on. "It's mine." I held up my hand. "His and mine together." I grabbed my cart. "Go live your life now, Noelle. I'm going to do the same."

As I strode off to finish my shopping, I only looked back on her once. And I was relieved and strangely proud to catch her setting down her empty basket and striding out the door. Of course she'd remembered her umbrella.

When I got home, Rachel wasn't there in the kitchen waiting to greet me and take stuff out of my hands. While I was happy she wasn't hovering over me, worried I was going to leave and stick her with the rent, it was strange that she wasn't there with the water already boiling for the spaghetti I'd just bought. Rachel was a stickler about having dinner on the table at six.

"Hey Rach? Want me to start the water?" I called. When there was no answer, I went to her bedroom, wondering if she'd fallen asleep. She'd be pissed if I let her nap this late.

Her door was half closed, but I could hear her voice floating out from behind it. "—never been to a party." She paused, and I realized she was on the phone. "I'll definitely feel safe if you and Gabe are there, yeah."

Was she talking to Beau? Wait. Gabe?

I heard her shift on her bed and froze, but she didn't come to the door and catch me, so I was free to keep eavesdropping as she went on. "Is he doing—He is? Yeah, she's been a little bit messed up this week but I think...Right, no, but I definitely want to. You know—" She giggled then and I ached to know what Beau was saying on the other end of the line. "I still haven't tried every drink on the bar menu!" She laughed, a big full-throated sound I hadn't heard from her before. "Maybe Gabe would know. I know, but he'd know something about what it would feel like, right? He used to take pills all the time."

My heart thundered in my ears. Disgust made bile rise into my throat, but I swallowed it back down and forced myself to step away from Rachel's door.

I knew she'd been cutting loose, and I didn't blame her. I knew she felt like she had catching up to do, and I'd trusted that Beau would keep her safe while she did it. She could go to as many parties with him as she wanted, but why was Gabe going too? Bars were one thing, but going to a party where who knew what kind of drugs would be available...

What the fuck was he doing?

Fear made my hands shake. I watched them tremble with the anxiety that was building. Gabe couldn't go to a party like that. He'd be risking two years of hard work. What was Beau thinking, letting him—

"No," I said to myself. "This has nothing to do with you."

I hadn't realized I said it aloud until Rachel called out from her room. "Everly? How long have you been home?" She appeared at her door looking worried. "Sorry. I didn't hear you come in."

"It's fine," I said tightly.

"I'll go start the water. Thanks for going shopping."

I pressed my hands into my sides so she wouldn't see them shaking. "Don't worry about it," I said. "I'm not hungry."

"Are you sure? Hey, I'm going out with Beau again tonight. I wanted to let you know."

"Where are you headed?" I asked, a little too pointedly.

She caught my tone and got defensive. "Taylor from the Crown is having a fish bake to celebrate the opening of trout season. Beau caught a bunch today and is bringing them over."

"Sounds wholesome," I snarked.

Her eyes hardened. "It's a party, but Beau is good about helping me know my tolerance." She pronounced the word carefully, like she still wasn't used to using it.

"What else are you going to do?"

"I think that's it." She eyed me. "Why? Did you want to come? It's supposed to be fun. Apparently he does it every year and the whole town comes out—"

"I'm good," I interrupted. So much had changed in the past few months. There was a time when I would have given anything to be included in something like this. To be noticed and invited. Now the last thing I wanted was to be around a bunch of people while I watched the man I loved and hated in equal measure destroy himself. "You have fun without me," I told her, and closed my bedroom door to be alone.

Chapter Thirty-Seven

GABE

Taylor Graham's annual fishbake had to move inside because of the constant rain. Which meant that instead of spreading out on the lawn by the creek for a bonfire, we were packed into his small converted trailer shoulder to shoulder. It was so tight that when my phone rang for what felt like the millionth time today, I had to apologize to the person I jostled as I reached for it.

"Gabriel!" Kit sounded jubilant. "Everything is all lined up. Our ducks are not only in a row, they're arranged by size and height."

A buzzing sound started up in my head. Almost like the sound of an alarm.

Beau and Rachel were too close by for me to discuss this freely. "Hold that thought, Kit," I said as I nudged and squeezed my way through the crowd and out into the lashing rain. "I had to get myself somewhere I could talk."

"Can you talk now?"

I looked out over Taylor's lawn. Gray gloom hung over everything, matching my mood, and the thunder of the creek was all-consuming. Here and there, I could see washouts at the edge of Taylor's lawn, the swollen creek carrying off chunks of stolen land. The slope on the left-most edge where the bonfire was usually set up had completely flooded out and the wind carved little ripples across the top of the swirling brown surge.

It was not a pretty sight, but it still made me feel wistful. Wistful and homesick for a place I hadn't even left yet. "I can talk," I said, even though I knew he wanted to talk about the last thing I wanted to hear.

Beau and Rachel didn't know that I was considering this my going-away party. Nobody knew, because I hadn't had the guts to tell them, because I hadn't wanted to say it aloud and make it true. Part of me hoped I could disappear in the wee hours tomorrow morning without anyone seeing me go.

Without running the risk of having to say goodbye.

"Great," Kit said, sounding impatient. "You know I'd usually send a car, but—"

"I can drive myself," I interrupted curtly. I didn't want to hear about how my hometown was little more than a speck on the map. I felt a strange surge of pride for the place I'd only started to appreciate. "What time do you need me at the airport?"

The noise in my head grew as thunderous as the creek. Kit was talking in earnest now, laying out details and itineraries, but I heard none of it. Staring out at the rushing water, I wondered if I was imagining things or if the flood had crept even closer to the house as I stood here. I felt like it was coming for me, coming to sweep me under.

For months, all I'd wanted was to leave this place. Now that it was finally happening, why did I feel like I was drowning?

"Gabe? Are you there?" Kit asked.

I opened my mouth to answer him.

Then I pulled my phone away from my ear and deliberately ended the call.

The crush of bodies had packed even tighter. Over the sea of bobbing heads I saw Beau looking down, a fond smile on his face as he watched Rachel dance. She was stiff and awkward, but there was something about her graceless exuberance that was completely captivating. Beau certainly seemed to think so.

I started to move to them, then stopped, an ache in my chest opening up like a canyon across my heart. I didn't want to see the two of them happy like that, marveling in how they'd found each other. I'd had that. I'd fucking had exactly that, and I'd ended it. I'd ended it rather than risk having Everly end it for me when I told her I was leaving.

If that wasn't the definition of shooting yourself in the foot, I didn't know what else it could be. By rights I should be limping again.

A *whoop* went up from the people by the front door. A couple of guys walked in and I felt the slight rush of recognition, though I didn't know from where or why. Three guys, all skinny and pale. It was raining like a bitch outside, but I guessed that sheen on their skin was sweat and not water.

"Fuck," I murmured. My hands itched, fingers curling in, already gripping the imaginary pill bottle. My mouth flooded with saliva, ready to swallow them down dry. I knew these guys because they were me two years ago.

What's the harm? my racing brain wanted to know. Already I was making plans for how I could bliss out for the next few arduous hours. I'd wake up feeling shitty, but then I felt shitty sober too, so what was the difference? I could score a few pills off these dudes and skip the next few horrid hours, skip forward in time to where leaving was inevitable.

I'd almost convinced myself this was a good plan when I spotted Rachel.

Beau was turned away, talking to Taylor. He didn't see how Rachel was watching the three new arrivals in open fascination. To my horror, this sheltered and naïve girl just starting to break free of her past made a beeline for the pillheads.

"No!" I growled. In three steps , I'd intercepted her, catching her up in my arms before she could get their attention. "Rachel. No."

She fought like a panicked wildcat to get free and I let go of her before she started yelling. "Hey! Hey hey hey, it's okay. I'm sorry I grabbed you."

"What the hell is going on?" Beau was at her side in an instant. She hugged herself, taking deep breaths. "You can't fucking grab her like that, man!" he shouted. Beau never shouted. "It freaks her out."

I raked my fingers through my hair. "I'm sorry, Rachel." I felt about two inches tall. "Just...keep her away from the pillheads, okay? Don't open that door. You might never get it closed again."

Beau looked at me and then down at the calming Rachel. "I told you no," he said. "I'll take care of you when you want to drink, but nothing more than that."

"You don't get to tell me no," Rachel hissed. "You're not in charge of me. No one is."

"Fuck," I repeated, raking my hands through my hair again. "Look, I'm sorry, okay? I'm just—I need some air." I turned away from my brother, who was so busy arguing with Rachel he didn't notice when I headed back out into the rain.

Chapter Thirty-Eight

EVERLY

It was one of the few nights off I had these days, and I was spending it on the National Institute of Health website, searching the statistics on successful recoveries from opioid addiction with my heart in my throat.

I couldn't do this. Addicts died from relapses all the time. Even worse was when they start using again after recovery. They think they still have the same tolerance as they used to.

He might not love me, but I could still save him. First and foremost, I was a nurse. It was my job to save him.

I ran out into the rain with my hoodie zipped up to my neck, still skirting around the Acura. I was going to save him from himself, no more than that. I didn't need to remind him of how good he'd been to me before he turned into a complete dick.

But Grim. Fucking Grim. My car saw my stubborn pride and promptly punished me for it by carrying me only halfway to Taylor's house. Then he seized his opportunity. I slowed at a four-way stop, and Grim let out a dramatic death rattle and died.

"Seriously?" I shouted, slamming the heel of my hand into the dash again and again. "You were fixed, you fucking piece of shit! What the hell do you think you're doing?"

I turned the key again and again, knowing that I was only making it worse. With one last curse on his entire model year, I shoved the door open and stepped out into the lashing rain.

Taylor's house was another two miles away by road. But if I cut through Latham's farm there and then followed the creek downstream, I'd come out into Taylor's back yard. It was less than a mile.

I set out at a run.

My shoes squished, mud sucking at my feet and slowing me down. Within moments, my shoes were soaked through. It was close to eight o'clock now, and what little light still hung on through the dim gloom was fading fast. I tried to pick up my pace.

"Fucking hell, Gabe," I snarled through chattering teeth. In my mind I could perfectly see his face, that strong, straight nose, that sweet, mocking mouth, but my brain kept forcing me to imagine him slumped over, the pills scattered across his chest. "No," I moaned as I saw him choking on his vomit with no one around who knew how to take care of him like I did. "Fuck you, seriously," I groaned.

I was so intent on getting to him before my vision came true that I barely noticed where my feet were landing. They were already numb, so it took me until the water started lapping around my calves to realize that I was standing in the middle of a lake.

I blinked and stood still, trying to get my bearings. Where Latham's corn field should have been there was a sea of water. I swallowed as I turned in a circle, looking for a familiar landmark.

That's when I noticed the tug of a current at my feet.

"Shit," I hissed. My heart pounded in sick, terrified thuds. I wasn't in a lake.

I was in the creek.

The flood had buried the field, erasing everything familiar, even as the last bits of light bled from the sky.

"Okay. Okay. I'm okay," I said, but the water was up to my knees, rushing so fast it was hard to lift my foot without the current threatening to tear it out from under me. I shuffled in a tight circle and let out a little moan when I felt the first splash above my knee. My hands shook steadily as I tried to count five sounds I could hear, five things I could see, but the grounding technique for warding off a panic attack only made me more aware of how fucked I was right now. "Fuck!" I screamed as the current knocked me off balance. Mindless with fear, I started running, half sprinting, half swimming. "Help!" I shouted, my body bobbing and twisting in the water.

The current grabbed me and yanked me off my feet, sending me under. I choked and sputtered as I fought to keep my head above water, then screamed as something unseen in the water raked a long, deep scratch across my leg. I twisted and fought as the current dragged me to the deep water where the flood was moving fastest. I coughed and flung out blindly, and my fingers closed on a low-hanging branch. I grabbed on with all my strength as the creek swept my legs out from under me. "Help!" I cried again.

"Where are you?" came a voice, distorted and faint.

I could barely hear over the rush of the creek and the water in my ears, but I pulled myself higher on the branch, ignoring the scrape of the twigs on my arms. "Here! I'm here!" I shouted. There was an ominous *crack* and the branch dipped lower in the water. I screamed.

And then I was being pulled through the water. The current tugged at me, dragging me down and not wanting to let me go, but I was being wrenched upward as I clung to the branch. "Hold on, Everly. For god's sake, don't let go."

"Gabe?"

"Can you reach my hand?"

My vision swam with water and tears, so he appeared out of nowhere, a blurred shadowy shape of a man. But I'd know that voice anywhere.

I forced myself to let go of the branch and reach out my shaking hand. His fingers clamped down on my wrist. "I've got you," he cried. "Let go of the branch."

"No!" I shouted in panic. The fingers of my other hand were so cramped up, I couldn't have let go if I tried. "No, I can't!"

"You can." He sounded calm. So calm. The darkness was near total now, but it was almost as if I could see his eyes looking down at me, more green than hazel, and feel his lips brushing across mine. "I've got you," he said. "But you have to let go of the branch so I can haul us both back up here. Come on, Everly. Trust me."

I let go of the branch.

In one motion he swung his other hand up, bracing himself by grabbing on to the tree, and hauled me upward with the other hand. The branch swirled, caught in an eddy, then got sucked out into the current as my foot landed on the muddy, shifting bank. Gabe yanked me up, then wrapped his arm around my waist. I clung to him as he leaned hard against the tree. The sound of our panting, gasping breath was almost as loud as the creek itself.

Gabe held me, murmuring with his lips against my forehead, until my breath came easier. Then he pushed off against the tree and gave me a shove up the steep bank. With the last of my strength I clawed my way up to level ground and flopped onto my stomach. The rain pounded my back and washed the tears from my face.

"What the hell were you doing?" Gabe had climbed up after me and was now crouched down at my side. There was still light enough to see his face, but not enough to read his expression, and I couldn't tell from his voice whether he was scared or angry.

"Saving you," I croaked.

Chapter Thirty-Nine

GABE

I stared at this wild, stubborn, hysterical girl lying mud-soaked and shaking on Taylor's back lawn, and all I could think of was how much I wanted to kiss her.

But I was too busy shaking my head. "*You* were saving *me*? Baby, I think the exact opposite happened."

She didn't seem to notice the endearment. She sat up and hugged her knees to her chest. "Gabe, you can't do this. I don't care if you don't love me anymore. You can't go back."

My heart stalled. "How'd you find out about the show?"

She tilted her head to the side. "The show? No, I'm talking about the pills. The drugs. You can't go back to that. You're better now!"

I was falling. Head over heels and tumbling right back in love with her. If I was honest with myself, I'd never *not* been in love with her. I'd only been too chickenshit to deal with what that meant for us both. "Baby, no." I pulled my shaking, shivering, soaking wet girl into my arms. "I'm not on pills again. I'm not."

"Rachel said that—at this party—"

"There were some people scoring here. But I wasn't one of them." I pressed my lips against her forehead. "Was that really why you decided to wade into a creek during a flood warning? To knock the pills right out of my hands?" My heart was so big it crowded my chest.

"I was going to try and reason with you first, at least," she protested, burying her face into my chest.

"God, I love you so much," I sighed.

Her face tilted to mine and I covered her mouth and kissed her with all of my love. She wrapped her arms around my neck and kissed me back the way only Everly could. "I love you too," she sighed against my mouth. "Clearly." I felt her smile. "I wish I could see you right now."

"We're getting really good at kissing in the dark."

She hummed, a little noise of remembrance, and pulled back from me. "But why did you break up with me? I'm sorry I freaked out about Noelle. I'm sorry I didn't believe you. That was me. I see that. It was my own insecurity and I put it on you. But then—" She gulped back a sob. "You let me go so easily."

"That was me," I said quickly. "*My* insecurity." I held my breath and let it out again in a rush. It was time for the truth. She deserved it after wading into a flood to make sure I was safe. She deserved it after taking a risk like that for me. "I was breaking up with you then so you couldn't break up with me now."

"Why would I break up with you?"

"Because I was about to leave to start filming King of Pain again."

"When?" I couldn't see her face, but I could hear the horror in her voice.

I was the biggest piece of shit on the planet. "Tomorrow."

"What the fuck? Gabe! Are you seriously going back to doing that daredevil shit?"

"*That daredevil shit* helped drag you out of a creek just now," I pointed out. "But who are you yelling? You went charging off into a flood to save me instead of, oh, I dunno, calling my brother or your housemate and asking them if I was okay." I grinned like a fool. God, I loved her so much. "Which one of us is the real daredevil?"

"But Gabe...tomorrow?"

I kissed her.

I kissed her slow enough and long enough that the rain started to lighten. When I finally pulled back, it was with new clarity. "I won't go," I declared.

"Of course you will," she said. "But not tomorrow."

"What?"

"Can you give me 'til I re-take my boards?"

"Everly?" Hope thudded in my chest.

"If you're gonna risk yourself like that, you're gonna need a nurse. I'll come with you once I have my license."

I felt so light I could float away. I was higher than I'd ever been before. "Seriously, baby? You can do whatever you want as long as you say you're mine."

"I'm yours," she said, pressing her hand to my heart. She smiled against my lips. "Glad you finally noticed," she said, and kissed me again.

EPILOGUE

Everly

I passed my boards.

It was strange how that was almost the least exciting part of those hectic weeks. Gabe's producer was none too pleased about having to reschedule the crew a second time, but Gabe managed to placate him by agreeing to do a few viral promo spots for free. Which meant I had to watch my boyfriend go hurtling across the muddy dirt track outside of town where he'd apparently broken his arm last winter, and I had to bite my tongue when he and Finn went kayaking down the flood-choked creek while a crew filmed them from the bridge in the middle of town.

Instead of hiding my eyes behind shaking hands, I found myself waving and cheering with the rest of the town as the two King brothers shot under the bridge and came out the other side.

Then there was the flurry of preparing to leave home for months on end. Rachel refused to sublet my room, wary of who would end up taking it. There had been whispers that the Chosen were pissed that she was living openly in town, "flaunting" herself the way she was. So I ended up fronting her two months of my half of the rent and making Beau promise to keep an eye on her. He agreed in his usual solemn way, even though the two were still fighting about how much of the secular world Rachel should be allowed to experience.

Then came informing my family that I was leaving the country to go travel the world with my daredevil rockstar boyfriend. Maybe I was chicken for telling all three of them via a Skype call instead of stopping by the house, but I had the satisfaction of seeing my mother sneer on one side of the screen while Abriella whooped and hollered on the other.

My Dad told me to watch out for Godzilla.

Then there was only one thing left to do before Gabe and I headed off for the two months of shooting.

"You know, this bar has seen pretty much every important night in our relationship, and you don't even drink," I observed as Gabe and I sat in the Crown Tavern and accepted everyone's well-wishes. Our going-away party was in full swing, and I was giddy with excitement.

"Yeah, baby. We need to branch out a little." Gabe squeezed my hand.

"Isn't that what we're doing tomorrow?"

"Damn straight."

"Riding dune buggies in the Sahara," I sighed. "That's gonna be a switch."

"Yeah, maybe we'll finally get out of the rain," Gabe said wryly.

"It was sunny today," I reminded him. "It finally came out to see us off."

"Hey, guys!" Rachel shouted. She held a drink in her hands. From across the room, Beau watched her, his expression unreadable. "I can't believe you're leaving, Everly!"

I laughed as she squeezed me tight. "You know I'll be back. It's only a few months."

"But who's going to teach me about secular life?" she moaned dramatically.

I gently took the drink from her hand. "I'm clearly a bad influence. How much have you had?"

"Nothing! It's just iced tea!" she slurred.

Gabe and I exchanged a look. "What kind of iced tea?" Gabe asked Rachel.

"Shit," I muttered, catching Beau's eye. "Watch her," I mouthed.

He nodded and I sagged against Gabe. "I feel like a bad friend. I'm the one who gave her her first drink."

"Beau's watching out for her," he said, lifting my hand to his lips. "Believe me, my brother is really good at watching out for people."

I pressed my lips together as Rachel stumbled to the front door. Beau was off his chair like a shot, hurrying after her. "I like your brother," I said.

"You like my brothers in general, I think," he teased, elbowing me in the ribs.

"Ass," I said, shoving him back. "I think I picked the best one." I grinned at him. "Eventually."

He threw back his head and laughed. "Told you—you have terrible taste in King Brothers."

"I have the best taste," I protested.

His hazel-green eyes met mine. "You're spectacular, you know that?"

"I do because you keep telling me."

"I'm gonna keep telling you every day from now on. Life is an adventure, baby, and we're gonna share it. Are you ready?"

I wrapped my arms around him, my heart dancing with excitement. "Ready as I've ever been."

THE END

BOOKS BY THERESA LEIGH

The Crown Creek Series

The Kings

Sweet Crazy Song

Jonah and Ruby's story

Cocky Jonah never wanted to come home to Crown Creek. But a chance meeting with kindergarten teacher Ruby has him wanting to stay forever.

Lost Perfect Kiss

Gabe and Everly's story

A risk taking bad boy. A girl-next-door nurse. And the kiss that never should have happened. Gabe has to convince Everly to take the biggest risk of her life. Him.

Soft Wild Ache

Beau and Rachel's story

Growing up in a repressive religious cult meant that Rachel always believed the outside world was evil. But when sensitive rocker Beau opens her eyes to life outside the compound walls, she learns that he's the sweetest sin she's ever seen.

His Secret Heart

Finn and Sky's story

Sky was certain she knew everything she needed to know about volatile, unpredictable bad boy Finn King. But when her world turns upside down, she realizes everything she thought she knew is wrong.

Crown Creek Standalones:

Last Good Man

Cooper and Willa's story

Willa hates Cooper. But when she wakes up in a hospital room, he's the one who's there waiting - rumpled, frantic... And swearing she's his fiancee.

Coming soon:

Ryan and Naomi's story

Sadie's story

Visit theresaleighromance.com for more.

ABOUT THE AUTHOR

Theresa Leigh is a romance author whose love of reading is so intense, she sometimes injures herself by walking around with her nose in a book. She loves writing stories that have you feeling every emotion... sometimes all on the same page.

Theresa lives and writes in the beautiful Finger Lakes region of New York State (not the city) (that distinction is important to her), where she lives with her husband, twin sons and twin orange cats, Pumpkin and Jackie O'Lantern. When she's not writing or reading, she enjoys eating too much Thai food, walking around barefoot, and cooing baby talk at her cats.

Get in touch!

www.theresaleighromance.com

authortheresaleigh@gmail.com

facebook.com/booksbytheresaleigh

Made in the USA
Lexington, KY
29 November 2019